The BIG KERPLOP!

The BIG KERPLOP!

The Original Adventure of the Mad Scientists' Club

Bertrand R. Brinley

PURPLE HOUSE PRESS
Texas

Published by
Purple House Press
Keller, Texas

Library of Congress Cataloging-in-Publication Data

Brinley, Bertrand R.
The Big Kerplop! : the original adventure of the Mad Scientists' Club
/ by Bertrand R. Brinley; illustrated by Charles Geer.—1st ed.
p. cm.
Summary: Seven boys organize the Mad Scientists' Club to investigate a
mysterious object dropped by an Air Force bomber into Strawberry Lake.
ISBN 1-930900-22-8 (alk. paper)
[1. Science clubs–Fiction.] I. Geer, Charles, ill. II. Title.
PZ7.B78013 Bi 2003
[Fic]–dc21   2002156152

www.PurpleHousePress.com

Printed in the United States of America
1 2 3 4 5 6 7 8 9 10
First Edition

This book is dedicated to Vercingetorix, a ten-year-old mackerel tabby cat, who specializes in laying ambushes for other cats in the house and who has slept on—or otherwise left his mark on—every page of the original manuscript except the last page, which I snaked from the typewriter and slipped into a folder just in time to spoil his record.

Introduction

Harmon Muldoon is quite a character. He falls overboard, ruins the fishing, makes a fool of himself, is a general pain in the neck, but quotes Shakespeare. Oddly enough, Harmon was once a friend of Jeff Crocker and Charlie, and it is their fishing trip that starts the original adventure of the Mad Scientists' Club.

As you read about how Jeff, Harmon and Charlie try to locate the mysterious object that drops in Strawberry Lake and ruins the fishing, you will meet others who appear time and again in the many tales of the Mad Scientists of Mammoth Falls. Henry Mulligan, of course, plays a big role in finding the object and helping the Air Force recover it. But it is Homer Snodgrass who suggests enlisting his help to start with. We encounter Homer on the sidewalk in front of his father's hardware store, where Jeff, Harmon and Charlie are pitching pennies. The idea for this came from the Twenties, when my father lived in Hollywood and sold newspapers, and often pitched pennies with Jackie Cooper, the child star. Freddy Muldoon and his sidekick Dinky Poore make their appearance, as does Mortimer Dalrymple, the electronics wizard.

But the big difference in this story is the amount of time some selected adults play on stage. We meet a couple of reporters who figure in the story. One of them must have been based on the many reporters my father worked with in a long career in press relations. Incidentally, besides giving you portraits of a solid reporter or two, *The Big Kerplop!* isn't such a bad primer in press relations. It is a guide on how to handle the press in a crisis, laced with subtle do's and don'ts.

Another adult who plays a big role is Colonel March, the base commander at Westport Field. Familiar to

Mad Scientists' Club readers, this time he is the man on the spot. And, when the incident becomes national news, he finds himself under pressure from the town, the press and Washington. My father knew officers like Colonel March in his military career; but a great deal of how the colonel handles himself under pressure in this crisis is my father himself.

The role of the adults in *The Big Kerplop!* alters the emphasis from the other twelve tales. This was inevitable from the start, because the original idea my father had for the story, which he entitled *The Sunken Village*, had the adults even more involved and Henry assuming a more political role. While the plots of *The Sunken Village* and *The Big Kerplop!* parallel each other in the early chapters, the later chapters in *The Sunken Village* are much more complex, involving considerable political controversy in the town.

My father first committed the idea of the underwater village to paper in a synopsis in 1968, while he was finishing the last of the individual stories, *The Great Confrontation*. As time went on though, his idea changed, judging from his notes. One set of notes laid out a series of alternatives for *The Sunken Village*, including two notions that in the end became *The Big Kerplop!* What influenced him to change his mind? That is hard to say. His editor and agent certainly; but perhaps other factors as well, as it took him two or three years to get back to writing what he had started in 1969.

What emerged finally in the book you have in your hands harkens back to the thread that runs through the tales of the Mad Scientists of Mammoth Falls: by using your noodle you can solve most problems. Jeff, Harmon and Charlie do a pretty good job of locating the area where the object is by using basic orientation skills. When Henry joins them, he solves one problem after another by thinking and applying scientific principles to find the solution. Now, he does need some help along the way; particularly in the person of the world-famous geologist, Professor Stratavarious.

The professor is based on a hilarious character that used to appear on Sid Caesar's comedy hour in the 1950s. Sid Caesar played the professor, who was usually sitting in a big leather armchair and constantly trying to keep from sliding down onto the floor. His monologue was interrupted by his accusations that someone was waxing the leather. The professor spoke with a heavy accent, which was part of the humor of the character. My father captured the accent and mannerisms pretty accurately in Professor Stratavarious.

A character who played a minor role in *The Big Kerplop!* was a real one: Vercingetorix. He was named by my father for the great Celtic warrior of Roman times. Verse (his nickname) was a mackerel tabby with black stripes on grey, and was probably my father's favorite cat after Effie (short for Iphigenia before we discovered that Effie was a boy) who stayed in Staten Island when the family moved to Florida. Verse would sit on a chair near a high-traffic area in the house and swipe at dogs, cats, people, etc., who walked by. I am not surprised that he got on every page of the manuscript save one. I have another manuscript containing a page he mistook for a scratching post. Great cat.

As I was writing this introduction, it occurred to me that this is the last Mad Scientists' Club tale set in Mammoth Falls. The next tale of the junior geniuses from Mammoth Falls takes them thousands of miles away. I also realized that a hankering for times past emerges, as Charlie recounts the glories of the Bristol Hotel and the Mammoth Falls Arms. The passage about the Bristol is pure nostalgia from our days in Vienna when my father and mother were young and very active socially at a historical time following World War II. They regularly met and socialized with diplomats, top American and Allied officers and officials, Congressmen and Senators, and many others who either passed through or were stationed in Vienna. The Bristol Hotel was often the site of receptions, dinners and similar events. It is still there, opposite the opera house.

A note about another aspect of the history of this book. When it was originally issued in 1974, the publisher was having financial problems, and only 1000 or so copies were ever distributed. That is why, until now, the book has been so rare. We hope that this edition, with large portions of original text restored, will make it possible for many, many more readers to share the original adventure of the Mad Scientists' Club.

Sheridan Brinley
Arlington, Virginia
2003

The BIG KERPLOP!

Contents

The Big Kerplop!

A lot of people have asked me how the Mad Scientists' Club first got organized. And I usually ask them, "What do you mean, organized?" Things like our club don't really get *organized*. They just sort of happen.

I guess if I had to pick a day the whole thing got started, I'd have to pick that creepy, overcast, fogbound day that Jeff Crocker and I made the mistake of asking Harmon Muldoon to go fishing with us on Strawberry Lake. That was the day of the big B-52 bomber scramble at Westport Field, when a mysterious object plopped into the lake and set in motion a chain of events that nobody in Mammoth Falls will ever forget.

As things turned out, the thing didn't really do much harm—like killing anybody, for instance—but it sure ruined the fishing for a week. And it set the whole town of Mammoth Falls on its ear for most of a month. But let me tell you how it all got started.

There is something about Harmon Muldoon that is just plain bad news. Not that he means to cause trouble; but, he just breeds it, wherever he is. We hadn't been out on the lake for more than fifteen minutes before he was digging into the lunch that we'd stowed under the stern seat of the boat so it would keep dry and not smell too fishy when we ate it.

"Excuse me, Harmon," said Jeff, pulling a crab with his right oar just in time to add a mouthful of water to the sandwich Harmon was biting into. "I just thought that peanut butter might be a little dry."

Harmon choked and sputtered, and coughed up half of the mouthful he was trying to swallow. His eyes bugged out, and his face got so red I thought he would burst a blood vessel. He started to say something, and that made him choke some more. He couldn't swallow what was in his mouth without choking, and he couldn't cough with his mouth full, so he ended up spitting it all out over the gunwale.

"Jeepers! I didn't think you'd get seasick so soon," Jeff taunted him.

Harmon started fumbling around for a handkerchief while he coughed some more, and managed to drop the rest of the sandwich into the bilge water in the bottom of the boat. It quickly turned into a sodden mass. I busted out laughing, and that made Harmon all the madder. He grabbed what was left of the sandwich and flung it the length of the boat at me. His aim was good, and the biggest part of it splattered against the left side of my neck. But his foot must have slipped, because I heard a loud guffaw just as the soggy sandwich slapped against my neck. And when I looked up, Harmon was no longer in the boat. He had catapulted over the stern and into the lake.

"Hey! Get out of there, Harmon, you'll poison the fish!" Jeff yelled at him. We were both laughing when he surfaced and started flailing his way back to the boat. He put both hands on the gunwale and started to pull himself over the side.

"Knock it off, you ninny," Jeff yelled at him, slapping one of his hands with the blade of an oar. "You board a boat over the stern, not over the side. You wanna capsize the boat?"

"I would, except it might get the rest of the lunch wet," Harmon sputtered, as he eased himself hand-over-hand around to the stern.

We helped him climb in and wring his wet clothes out, and Jeff gave him a towel to rub down with.

"Are you cold?" Jeff asked him. "Your teeth are chattering."

"That ain't my teeth," Harmon said, scornfully. "That's just the rocks in your head rattling."

"Very funny!" I said. "But your lips are turning blue."

"They should be. I'm swearin' a blue streak under my breath."

One thing about Harmon: he's like the India Rubber Man in the circus—he snaps back in a hurry. I tossed him a heavy canvas tarpaulin I dug out of the storage locker in the prow of the boat and told him to put it over him until his clothes got dry. When you're cold and wet there's nothing like a clammy, mildewed tarpaulin right next to your skin. Harmon sat there with it draped over his shoulders and tried his best to look dignified. There wasn't a chance in the world of his clothes drying out, unless the sun broke through the overcast. And just then it was so foggy we couldn't see more than fifty feet from the boat.

Jeff and I set about baiting hooks and putting sinkers on our lines while Harmon sat shivering in the stern seat. We figured the large-mouthed bass and the wall-eyed pike Strawberry Lake is famous for would be hitting pretty good in the fog. There was no wind, and it was still and quiet on the lake.

We handed Harmon a rod, but he just sat there with his knees knocking together, letting the end of it dip into the water. Harmon just doesn't have the temperament for fishing. Fishing takes a great deal of patience and a lot of quiet contemplation. If you can't contemplate, you might as well not try fishing. Harmon is too nervous for that. If something isn't happening every minute, he wants to make something happen.

We hadn't had our lines in the water for more than five minutes when he turned on the radio he'd brought with him.

"Turn that thing down," Jeff muttered between clenched teeth. "You'll scare the fish away."

"Go blow your horn," said Harmon. "Music is good for the soul."

"We're not fishing for sole, lunkhead, we're fishing for bass."

"Oh, you're a real panic!" Harmon snorted. "How come you're not on TV?" And instead of turning the volume down, he turned it up.

Just as he did, the program was interrupted for a public service announcement. The Air Force had scheduled a practice alert for the strategic bomber squadron stationed at Westport Field, the announcer said, and jet aircraft would be taking off from the field intermittently during the next two hours in flights of four or five.

"Holy Mackerel!" I groaned. "There goes the fishing for the morning."

"I thought you were fishing for bass," Harmon grunted.

Jeff and I looked at each other and shrugged our shoulders. We just sat there for a while, hoping we would get a few strikes before the scramble started. If anything, the fog was getting thicker, and if we were going to go in early we'd have to use Jeff's compass to get back to shore. We really didn't know exactly where we were, but that didn't matter much. We knew that the bombers always took off on a heading that took them right out over the water, so they could head for the gap in the hills at the northwest corner of the lake where all the swamps and marshes are. When they passed over us, they'd only be a couple of hundred feet in the air, and the noise and shock waves would drive all the fish to the bottom.

"If we can't fish, why don't we eat lunch?" Harmon suggested.

"Is that all you think about?" Jeff asked him. "It's a wonder you're not as fat as your cousin Freddy."

"There's a difference," Harmon explained. "Freddy just lives to eat. I eat to live. And I burn it all off, so it doesn't go to fat."

"Must be a pretty slow burn," I said. "Or is that a money belt you wear around your waist?"

Just then we heard the pulsating roar of the first bomber rumbling over our heads. We all ducked instinctively. The sound was so magnified in the dense fog that the huge plane seemed to be not more than

twenty feet above us. We crouched in the boat with our
mouths open and our fingers in our ears.

"Whew-w-w!" Jeff whistled. "The wind from that
one parted my hair. I hope they have their landing gear
retracted by the time they get to us."

We sat there for a while longer, trying to make up our
minds whether to head for shore and give up on fishing
for the day. Three more planes thundered over our
heads, each one seeming to create a more deafening
bombardment of shock waves than the one that pre-
ceded it. The smell of JP-4 was everywhere around us.

"Whew, that stinks!" said Harmon. "I don't know
about the fish, but it sure ought to make the mosqui-
toes scarce."

"There'll probably be one more in this flight," Jeff
declared. "Then maybe it'll be quiet long enough for
the fish to come back."

"Maybe we ought to rig our lines for deeper water,"
I told Jeff. "This racket covers the whole lake, and the
only place the fish can go is down toward the bottom."

"You're right," Jeff answered. "Let's pull 'em in."

Just as we were reeling in, the fifth plane in the
flight came roaring at us, setting up a high-pitched
clatter of sound that made the boat vibrate.

"That boy's in trouble!" shouted Harmon.

"Yeah! He's got a problem," Jeff shouted back, as the
blast from the plane's engines tailed off in the distance.

Whatever the problem was, it landed in the lake
with a loud *KERPLOP!*

It was so close to us you could almost feel the force
of the splash. But the fog was so thick we couldn't see
a thing.

"Jumpin' Jehoshaphat!" Harmon shouted. "They're

bombin' us!"

"Keep your skin on, bathing beauty," Jeff cautioned him. "And stay in your seat."

Then the boat began to rock, and we knew that whatever had hit the water was large enough to set up wave fronts two or three feet high.

"Man the oars!" I shouted to Jeff, and he grabbed them in time to turn the nose of the boat into a wave big enough to capsize us. We sat there pitching up and down for a few seconds, and then Jeff started pulling slowly toward the source of the disturbance. Harmon had forgotten all about being cold and was half-standing, half-kneeling, half-naked on the stern seat, peering into the fog.

"Maybe his bomb bay doors busted loose," he said.

"It was heavier'n that," Jeff grunted, between pulls at the oars. "More like a whole tail section."

Finally the boat stopped pitching and we found ourselves in smooth water. But there was nothing to be seen except some air bubbles breaking the surface of the lake. Whatever hit the water had long since sunk out of sight.

"*Sic transit gloria* something-or-other!" Harmon proclaimed from his perch in the rear. And he flung the tarpaulin grandly over his left shoulder.

"You can say that again!" Jeff murmured, half out of breath.

"I would, but I can't remember the words," Harmon chuckled.

"Look, wise guy, you better keep that tarp over your shoulders or you'll catch one dilly of a cold," Jeff warned. "Now, fish or no fish, I think we'd better head back for shore. Whatever fell off that bomber may be something the Air Force wants to recover, and maybe we can give them a clue as to where it is."

"Give them a clue?" Harmon snorted. "It's obvious where it is. It's right there!" And he pointed to where the bubbles were still rising to the surface.

Jeff groaned. "Okay, fathead! Maybe you'd like to step over there and tread water for a while so we'll know where to look when we get back out here."

"Look out who you're callin' 'fathead'!" Harmon exclaimed, swinging his wet pants at Jeff's head.

Jeff pushed him back in his seat with the butt of an oar.

"Sit down and listen to me," he said. "We don't know where we are, and we can't see the shoreline from here. If we want to find this spot again, or come anywhere close to it, we've got to use our noodles. Now, we're going to row back to shore on a compass heading so we know what direction to take to find this spot again; and we're going to count how many strokes it takes to get there, so we have some idea of the distance. You get up front, Harmon, and count the strokes. Charlie, you sit in the stern and handle the compass."

Jeff has a no nonsense way about him that makes everybody listen to him when he talks. He doesn't ever throw his weight around, but whenever there's a tight situation, people just naturally follow his directions. I took the compass from him and put another oar in the stern oarlock to steer with. We headed off due northeast on a compass bearing of 45 degrees. Jeff didn't choose this heading by accident. For one thing, he figured it would bring us to shore at about the point where Turkey Hill Road runs closest to the lake, and we could get to a telephone at a gas station if we wanted to. For another thing, it was approximately at right angles to the flight path of the planes taking off in the scramble, and this might give the Air Force a pretty good fix on the location of whatever dropped into the lake.

With Jeff rowing steadily, we reached a point on the shore a little to the west of where we expected, but we got there a lot sooner than we thought we would.

"I guess we weren't as far out as I thought," Jeff said. "We must have drifted quite a bit while Harmon was taking his bath."

We hadn't heard any more planes taking off, and though Harmon had kept his radio turned on all the time we hadn't heard any more announcements about the practice alert.

"Seems funny," Harmon commented. "If that plane was in trouble, you'd think they'd have made some announcement about it. And, if it wasn't, how come there's no more planes taking off?"

"Maybe they stopped for a coffee break," I suggested.

"Don't be a nut!"

"Well, it's your question. You answer it."

Jeff had made his way up the shoreline to where he could get onto Turkey Hill Road and find a telephone. When he got back we asked him what was up.

"I don't know what's going on," he said. "They wouldn't tell me anything."

"Did you tell 'em we saw something drop in the lake?"

"I told them we *heard* something drop in the lake, and this man I talked to said, 'Thanks. We'll check into it,' and that was all. He didn't even ask me my name, or anything."

"Who was it you talked to?" I asked.

"Some sergeant at Westport Field. I don't know his name."

"That makes you even," Harmon chimed in. "He doesn't know yours, either. You shoulda talked to somebody in Flight Operations."

"That's what I asked for, but they said there was an alert on and they couldn't put any calls through to Flight Operations."

"Well, that's that," I said. "What do we do now?"

Jeff shrugged his shoulders and kicked up some sand. Then we all sat down on a log and chewed the matter over for a while. We all agreed that we should at least report what we knew to the Mammoth Falls police, and maybe they could report it to the Air Force. Harmon pointed out that if Westport Field was going to conduct a search for what was in the lake, they would have to work through the local police.

"You're right," Jeff observed. "We'd better go down to the station and do that right away."

"While we're there, I can run over to the *Gazette* and tell my uncle," Harmon added. "The paper oughta be interested."

"Good idea!" said Jeff. "Maybe they can find out what's going on."

We pushed the boat out into the lake again, and with Jeff and Harmon both at the oars we headed for the dock down the eastern shore of the lake where Jeff's folks have their summer cottage. I was sitting in the stern seat manning the steering oar and pondering the mystery of what fell into the lake, when an idea struck me that was so elementary I wondered why we hadn't thought of it in the first place.

"Hey, you guys!" I blurted out. "I got another idea!"

"Another idea?" Harmon puffed. "When did you have the first one?"

"Never mind smartin' off, Harmon. I haven't heard any brain-busters comin' out of you!"

"You have to have a brain to recognize a brain-buster when you hear one," he retorted.

"All right, all right, you guys!" Jeff interrupted. "Let's hear it, Charlie."

"Well, it's simple," I said. "Why don't we go get our scuba gear and get back out there and find out what's at the bottom of the lake?"

There was a pause while Jeff looked at Harmon, and Harmon looked at Jeff, and they both turned and looked at me.

"Boy! Why didn't I think of that?" Harmon muttered.

"Great idea, Chazz," Jeff said, hesitantly. "But we don't know how deep it is out there. It may be beyond our depth."

"We'll never find out unless we try!" I shot back.

"Yeah...I guess you're right," Jeff admitted. "C'mon. What are we waiting for?"

"Yeah, man! Let's make waves!" Harmon crowed. He and Jeff started pulling water like a couple of one-man scull buffs.

We practically hydroplaned down the shoreline toward Jeff's dock, swapping ideas on how to get our stuff together as soon as possible and get back out on the lake. By the time we reached the dock, where we'd left our bikes, the fog showed signs of lifting, and our spirits rose even further. But, as it turned out, things would have been better if it had stayed socked in all day.

Jeff and I went straight to the police station in the

town square to make our report, while Harmon went to
see his uncle who operates a linotype machine in the
composing room of the Mammoth Falls *Gazette*. Then
we high-tailed it home to get our diving gear.

The town of Mammoth Falls isn't much. It's a small
town, as towns go these days, and it's kind of old-fash-
ioned. But it's a nice place to live. It has one big disad-
vantage, though. Almost everybody in town knows
almost everybody else; and what makes it worse, they
almost always know what everybody else is doing. So,
when we got back to Jeff's dock with our air tanks,
masks, and flippers, there was already a reporter there
from the *Gazette*, and one from one of the radio stations,
and a couple of the regular retainers from Ned Carver's
Tonsorial Parlor.

Harmon likes to talk, but Jeff doesn't; so there was a
little tug-of-war between them before we got all our
equipment into the boat, and Jeff and I had carried his
outboard motor out of the boathouse and clamped it
onto the transom of the fishing dinghy.

"C'mon, knucklehead!" Jeff shouted back at
Harmon, who was doing his best to tell everybody on
the dock what we were up to. "Let's get moving."

Harmon reluctantly broke away from the group on the
dock after promising a sensational revelation upon our
return, and clambered into the boat, where he immediately struck a dramatic pose in the prow. I started the
motor and revved it up good before I cut the clutch in,
so we shot away from the dock in a cloud of spray and
exhaust fumes, and Harmon toppled from his perch
and ended up flat on his back in the bilge.

"You're a real nut!" Jeff told him, as soon as we were
out of earshot. "We don't have any idea what dropped

from that plane. And even if it is something important, we don't know whether we'll find it. Why do you make stupid promises like that?"

"Horsefeathers!" Harmon fumed as he regained his stance in the prow and raised a clenched fist in the air. "There is a tide in the affairs of men, which, taken at the flood, leads onto fortune!" he shouted into the wind.

"It can also get you all wet!" Jeff shouted back. "Now get down in the boat before you get another dunking."

The fog was definitely lifting as I steered the boat along the shoreline toward the point near Turkey Hill Road where we had landed earlier. It only took us a few minutes to get there with the motor; but from that point on Jeff would have to row, because that was the only way we could tell how far out in the lake we should go.

"How many strokes did I take coming in?" Jeff asked.

"Four hundred and eighty-five-and-a-half, right on the schnozzola," said Harmon.

"Where did the 'half' come from?"

"You pulled a crab once. I counted it half a stroke."

"Okay! Let's get it right on the schnozzola again," said Jeff.

"Yes, sir, admiral!" said Harmon, giving Jeff a snappy salute.

"What's our heading, Charlie?"

"We came in on 45 degrees," I told him. "That means we go back out on 225 degrees. Right?"

"Right!" said Jeff, and he leaned into the oars.

I put the compass down on the seat in front of me and kept my eyes glued to it while I steered. With the needle bouncing back and forth it wasn't easy trying to keep the nose of the boat in line with 225 degrees. But a slight breeze had come up, and the fog was thinning rapidly, now. I hollered to Jeff to knock it off, and he let the oars drop.

"We aren't gonna make it this way," I told him. "Let's wait 'til this fog clears a bit, then maybe I can sight an azimuth to some point on the other shore over there. The way we're going I could be three hundred yards off and not know it."

"I guess you're right," Jeff agreed. "There's no sense in getting out there if we don't really know where we are."

He pulled back toward the shore, and we waited there for the fog to dissipate. It was only a few minutes before I could make out the outline of the ridge of hills on the west shore of the lake. As the fog drifted away I scanned the ridge carefully for some prominent feature we could home in on. While we were waiting, Harmon jumped ashore and broke off a dead branch of a tree, which he stuck upright in the sand. Then he draped a bright red jacket on it, which he had brought along in case it got cold, and clambered back into the boat.

"If we're gonna do this right, we have to know where we came from as well as where we're going," he explained. "That'll give us something to sight back on, so you can make sure we're going in a straight line."

"Good idea!" said Jeff. "You know, you may turn out to be useful after all, Harmon. That's the second brilliant thing you've done today."

"What was the first one?" Harmon asked.

"When you put your pants on this morning."

"Oh, you're very funny. Let's get going before I die laughing."

We started off again, with Jeff rowing and me steering. I kept the prow headed toward a sharp notch in the profile of one of the hills on the far shore where a patch of blue sky was already visible. It read exactly 225 degrees from our starting point. We made good progress until Harmon suddenly shouted from the bow seat.

"You're pulling too hard...ninety-four...Jeff. We'll overshoot the mark...ninety-five...by a mile if you keep this up...ninety-six!"

"Okay! Okay!" said Jeff, and he slacked off. "How's this?"

"That's fine...ninety-nine...that's fine."

For the first time that morning the sun burst through the overcast as Jeff back-paddled at the spot where Harmon finished his count. Only faint wisps of fog still drifted about when we dropped anchor in thirty feet of water. Jeff was amazed.

"I thought it was a lot deeper here than that!" he exclaimed.

"Yeah! Maybe there's an underwater ridge or a small hill right here," I said. "I've been told the lake's at least a hundred feet deep in this area."

"Well, we'll soon find out."

We had just gotten our air tanks and flippers on, and Harmon was already letting himself over the stern, when the staccato beating of whirlybird rotors echoed back and forth across the lake. From the direction of Westport Field two Air Force choppers were winging their way toward us, skimming low over the water.

"Maybe they're out looking for floating debris," said Harmon.

"From what we heard splash in the water, I don't think they'll find anything," Jeff declared. "Besides, they're flying too low to be searching for anything. You know, they seem to be heading straight for us!"

By the time they were half way out to us, there was no longer any doubt about it. They were homing in on our boat like it was a target. Harmon pulled himself back into the boat and we braced ourselves for the blast of air and sound we knew we'd get when they came close to us. The lead chopper climbed about fifty feet in the air, directly over us, and hovered there, while the second one came in as close to our starboard side as it dared and settled a few feet above the water like a big flapping hen. A man in a bright orange suit leaned out of the door hatch and started waving wildly at us. We smiled and waved back, saying "Hi! How ya fella? Nice day, isn't it?" and all sorts of inane things like that; but our voices were completely drowned in the tumult of noise and air turbulence surrounding us. The man cupped his hands to his mouth and shouted something, and we put our hands up to our ears and hollered, "What?" and "Can't hear you!" and shook our heads. Then he made broad, sweeping gestures with his left arm, pointing back toward the shore. We looked where he was pointing, but we couldn't see anything, so we shook our heads again.

"I think he's trying to tell us something," said Harmon Muldoon.

Jeff just looked at him with a scornful stare. "It could be that they think we're looking in the wrong place and want us to move in closer to shore," he ventured. Then Jeff tried some Indian sign language, but both the men in the chopper just looked blank.

"I think they're both palefaces," said Harmon.

Finally, the man who had been doing all the signaling

looked up at the second chopper and waved it away. Then the first one moved in even closer and hovered right over us. Now the sound was even more deafening, and we had to hold our fingers in our ears. The man scribbled a note on a piece of paper and threw it down, but it got caught in the blast from the rotors and sailed a hundred yards away before it settled onto the water. Jeff got hold of the oars and started rowing toward it. The whirlybird veered upward and peeled off to the right in the direction of Westport Field with the man in the orange suit waving his arm for us to follow him.

"I guess they want us to move in closer to shore," Jeff surmised. "But let's go get that note first."

We rowed to where we thought the note had dropped, and Harmon spotted it and snaked it out of the water. But the ink on it had turned to a blurry smudge and it was completely unreadable. By this time the chopper had circled back and was heading toward us again. It was about halfway back to us when it suddenly veered off, gained altitude, and headed straight for Westport Field. When the sound of its motor had died away, we heard another sound and realized why the chopper had left. A high-speed motorboat was coming toward us at full throttle from the direction of the public bathing beach. As it drew closer we realized it was the Mammoth Falls police launch that patrols the lake during the height of the boating season. It pulled up alongside us and Chief Harold Putney reached out and grabbed the gunwale of our boat.

"Sorry, boys, but you'll have to get off the lake," he said in his usual calm fashion. "You'd better follow us back toward the bathing beach."

"Why? What's up, Chief?" Jeff asked him.

"I don't know any more than you do," the chief answered. "All I know is that Colonel March called me and said he had some kind of emergency and asked me to clear the lake and keep people off the beaches. Probably has something to do with that alert they're having. Maybe they've got a plane in trouble. I don't really know."

"I think we know!" Harmon volunteered. "We were out here fishing when the scramble started, and we heard something big drop in the lake."

"The desk sergeant told me about that, but I wouldn't spread that around too much until we really know what happened," the chief warned.

"Oh we won't! Don't worry!" Harmon promised, not bothering to mention that he'd already told his uncle, so everybody on the newspaper knew about it.

Jeff started the motor up and we followed the police launch back to the beach. Chief Putney agreed to let us go on up the shore to the dock at Jeff's cottage, where we had left our bicycles, and we noticed that other policemen and sheriff's deputies were checking the cottages all along the beach to see if there were any people in them.

"Whatever's going on, it must be important," Jeff said. "Turn on your radio, Harmon, and let's get into town and see if we can find out what's happening."

"Maybe that was a real, live bomb that dropped in the lake!" I said.

"If it was, maybe we'll see some excitement," Harmon added. "Hey, Jeff, what'll we do with all our diving gear?"

Jeff thought for a minute. "Maybe it's better if we take it up to my barn. We don't know what's going on, and if they're keeping people away from the beaches, we may not be able to get back here when we want it."

As it turned out, this was a good thought. But then, Jeff usually makes the right decision. That's why all the kids at school call him "Old Reliable," and that's why he's captain of the baseball team and the basketball team.

When we got back into town you could tell something unusual had happened. The town square seemed to have more people in it than usual, and there were several state police and county sheriff's cars parked in front of the Town Hall, as well as two Air Force sedans and an Air Police vehicle. The radio station had just announced that the bomber alert had been terminated, and the Air Force had asked all stations to warn citizens to stay away from the vicinity of Strawberry Lake. It was assumed that some sort of accident had occurred, the announcer said, but they were awaiting further details from the Air Force.

We decided to split up and see what we could find out, and then meet at the Town Hall, which seemed to be the center of activity. Harmon went to the *Gazette* offices, while I went to Ned Carver's barber shop, where most everybody goes if they want to find out what's going on in town. Jeff decided to nose around the police station some, on the pretense that he wanted to find out if they had checked up on the report we had given them earlier in the morning. We met back at the steps of the Town Hall about ten minutes later to compare notes.

Harmon reported that the *Gazette* offices were busy as a beehive, sending reporters and cameramen out to the air base and to the Town Hall, and any place else they thought they might get some information. They

were pretty sure a major accident had happened, but
they had no idea what. The Air Force was being awfully
cagey, a friend of Harmon's told him, and the editor
was on the phone to Washington right then, trying to
see if he couldn't get some information cracked loose
from Westport Field.

"They took my picture while I was there, too," he
said, a little sheepishly.

"What for?" Jeff asked him.

"Because I told 'em all about what we heard, and
about gettin' kicked off the lake."

"I thought Chief Putney asked you not to spread that
around?"

"I mean before...when I was in there this morning.
I sure wouldn't tell 'em nothin' now."

"What about Jeff and me?" I asked Harmon. "Don't
they want our pictures, too?"

"I told 'em you was there, too," said Harmon, "but
they didn't say nothin' about takin' your pictures."

Jeff looked at me, and I looked at him, and we both
looked at Harmon as if he was a worm, or something.
But Harmon had decided it was time to blow his nose,
and he wouldn't look straight at us.

"What about the police station?" I asked Jeff. "What
did you find out there?"

"Zilch!" said Jeff. "*Positively* zilch!" he added, giving
the fire hydrant at the curb a kick with the side of his
foot.

"Same here!" I said. "Everybody in the barber shop
was asking me what I knew. They're all just listening to
the radio."

"I wonder what the Air Force is doing here," Harmon
said, jerking his head toward the entrance to the Town

Hall. "Maybe we could sneak inside and find out."

"Fat chance," said Jeff. "They're not letting *anybody* in."

And he was right. Constable Billy Dahr was blocking the entrance, and even the reporters from the *Gazette* and the radio stations had been told to stay outside on the steps. All they had been able to find out was that Colonel March, the commanding officer at Westport Field, was meeting with the mayor and the members of the Town Council.

"The mayor will probably make an announcement when he's ready," Constable Dahr assured them.

But Constable Dahr hadn't reckoned with Abner Sharples, who is one of the more loud-mouthed members of the Town Council. No sooner had he gotten the words out, than Abner came bursting through the door, shoved Billy Dahr aside, and proclaimed in a voice loud enough to be heard across the square, "THEY SAY THERE'S AN ATOM BOMB SOME-WHERE IN STRAWBERRY LAKE!"

The reporters clustered around him, all asking questions at once. But Abner pushed his way through them and dashed down the steps, two at a time.

"Hey! Where are you going, Councilman?" they shouted after him.

"I just remembered I have to take my family up to Great Bear Lake for a week!" Abner flung back at them, as he high-tailed it up the street and disappeared around a corner.

Night Venture

Abner Sharples was gone. But the words he left behind him still seemed to hang in the air, and in a moment they had fanned out through the town like a spreading wildfire. People were not quite sure what they had heard, but they repeated it anyway. And I hardly have to tell you what happened.

Have you ever played the game of *Gossip*? It's a great game for parties. You just seat about twenty people around a table and have one of them whisper a simple sentence into the ear of the person next to him. After this sentence has been whispered from ear to ear around the table, you compare what the twentieth person heard, with what the first person actually said—and the result is usually hilarious. Sometimes it's downright embarrassing. It tickles the ear a little bit, but it's a great game.

Something like the game of *Gossip* happened that afternoon in the town square of Mammoth Falls. By the time Abner's words had reached Walnut Street, there was not only an atom bomb in the lake, but it had already exploded and the town was being blanketed with radioactive dew. By the time they reached Mike Corcoran's Idle Hour Pool Hall on Blake Street, Russia had declared war on the United States and the National Guard was being mobilized.

The reporters, who had shouted vainly after the retreating figure of Abner Sharples, turned in a body and practically exploded through the door of the Town Hall, heading for the Council chambers. A litter of notebooks and microphones, left in their wake, covered the prostrate body of Constable Billy Dahr.

Harmon Muldoon burst out laughing. But Jeff and I ran up the steps and helped Billy Dahr get back on his feet. I grabbed his hat and billy club and handed them back to him. And then I made a big thing out of helping him brush the dust off his trousers while Jeff nipped inside the door to join the reporters. It was an old trick, but it was wasted. No sooner had Jeff gotten inside, than he found himself being ushered outside again by Chief Harold Putney, who was herding the reporters back out to the front steps.

"If you'll wait here a moment, gentlemen, the mayor will have an announcement for you," he said, firmly. "Now, please be patient."

There was some grumbling among the reporters, but they waited patiently enough until Chief Putney stepped away from the door to let the members of the Town Council come out onto the steps. Mayor Alonzo Scragg led the group, with Colonel March from Westport

Field at his side. The mayor was immediately surrounded by the reporters from the radio stations, who thrust long, skinny microphones into his face.

"Gentlemen!" said the mayor, in a high-pitched, squeaky voice. "I have an announcement to make." He cleared his throat three times and consulted some notes he was clutching close to his middle coat button. Then he looked up and gazed rather vacuously at the array of anxious faces confronting him.

"Yes, Mr. Mayor?" one of the reporters prompted.

"Er, yes," the mayor repeated. Then he took a rather deep breath and shuffled the notes in his hands. "Colonel Westport has told me...." he began.

"Do you mean Colonel March?" one of the reporters asked.

The mayor looked a little flustered for a moment. "Of course I mean Colonel March," he said rather testily. "I don't know a Colonel Westport." Then he laughed, nervously, and the reporters joined in.

"Colonel March has told me and the members of the Town Council that a strategic weapon has accidentally been jettisoned from one of the aircraft participating...."

"What do you mean by a strategic weapon?" he was asked.

Mayor Scragg appeared flustered again and turned to the colonel for help.

"The weapon is a nuclear device," the colonel stated matter-of-factly.

"You mean it's an atom bomb, Colonel?"

"I guess you could call it that, if you want to," the colonel admitted. "Actually, it's a nuclear device."

"The colonel assures me that it's a very small one, however," the mayor explained.

"How small?" asked the reporter from the *Gazette*.

At this point, Lieutenant Graham, the Information Officer from Westport Field, stepped forward. "The size of the device is classified, gentlemen," he said. "I suggest we let the mayor continue with his statement, and then we will answer questions—if it is possible to answer them within the limitations of national security." He nodded toward Mayor Scragg, who again held his notes up before him.

"A strategic weapon has accidentally been jettisoned from one of the aircraft participating in this morning's training exercise," he continued. "An object is *believed* to have fallen into the waters of Strawberry Lake. And I want to emphasize the word *believed*. We have no direct evidence at this time that the object is actually *in* the lake."

"We've got evidence!" Harmon Muldoon cried out, pushing his way into the group of reporters. "We heard it splash in the water and we know where it is."

"That's fine. That's just fine!" said Mayor Scragg, patting Harmon patronizingly on the head and pushing him back out of sight. "The Air Force will be conducting search and recovery operations in the vicinity of Strawberry Lake until the object is found," he continued. "Meanwhile, we have jointly taken steps to clear the area, and to prevent sightseers and curiosity-seekers from interfering with the search operation."

Then came the obvious question, "What about the danger of radioactivity?" from a chorus of voices. "What about fallout?" "Isn't this thing likely to explode before you find it?" "How do we know it's safe?"

Mayor Scragg backed off from the barrage of questions and looked toward Colonel March. The colonel nodded and stepped to the microphones.

"There is absolutely no danger of radioactivity, either in the waters of the lake, or in the surrounding atmosphere," he stated, positively. "I wish to assure the people of Mammoth Falls that adequate precautions have been taken, and are being taken, both in the design of the device and in the recovery procedures, to prevent any untoward incident from occurring. You can state unequivocally and categorically that there is no danger of harmful radiation."

"I hope that satisfies you gentlemen on that point," the mayor smiled. "And now, if you'll excuse me, I have other business to attend to, and I assure you that we will call another press conference as soon as we have further developments to announce." And with that, he strode through the knot of reporters and down the Town Hall steps to the sidewalk, where he glanced upward toward the sky. And even though the sun was now shining brightly, and it was a beautifully clear day, he unfurled his ancient, black umbrella and hoisted it over his head as he stalked off in the direction of Vesey Street. Before he had reached the corner, however, he paused and turned back toward the reporters. "I forgot one thing," he said, squinting at his crumpled notes. "The aircraft involved returned to its base without further incident."

Colonel March and Lieutenant Graham had taken advantage of the mayor's departure to move quietly toward the two Air Force sedans parked at the curb. They had almost reached the cars when the reporters recovered their senses and descended upon them in a body. One of them grabbed Lieutenant Graham's elbow.

"Excuse me, Lieutenant, but could you answer one more question?"

"Certainly!"

"If there is no danger of radioactivity, why are you keeping people away from the lake?"

"That's a good question!" said the lieutenant, looking toward Colonel March.

"Merely a precaution," the colonel answered from the back seat of his car. "We don't want anyone interfering with the search operations, and we don't want anyone to get hurt."

"What about this kid that says he knows where the bomb is, Colonel?" another reporter shouted.

The colonel smiled, tolerantly. "We'll be making a full investigation and questioning all possible witnesses if we have any difficulty in locating the device," he explained. And with that, his car pulled away from the curb and drove out of the square.

Harmon Muldoon gave the fireplug at the curb a vicious kick and howled in pain when he realized his big toe was sticking out through a hole in his sneakers. "Rotten old Air Force!" he complained. "If I busted my toe, I'll sue 'em!"

"Do you really know where that bomb is?" asked the man from the *Gazette*.

" 'Course we do!" Harmon blustered. "And we're gonna prove it to 'em, too," he added, shaking his fist in the direction of Colonel March's disappearing car.

"How do you plan to prove it?" questioned the newsman, with an amused wink at his fellow reporters.

Harmon started to open his big mouth again, but Jeff stepped in and grabbed him by the shoulders. "C'mon, Harmon, we're wasting our time here," he said. As we walked to where we had left our bicycles, we could hear the reporters wisecracking to each other while they dashed up the Town Hall steps to get to the telephone.

By the next morning, Mammoth Falls was big news all over the country. The Air Force had flown divers and special equipment into Westport Field late the previous afternoon, and they had worked until nightfall without any success in locating the bomb. Now, the town was in virtual turmoil. People who had some other place to go were packing up and leaving. The Town Hall and the Civil Defense Headquarters had been harassed all night by people wanting to know what they should do to protect their crops and animals. And the staff of the *Gazette* had been up all night answering requests for on-the-spot reports from newspapers and radio stations thousands of miles away. There was a good rumor going that the bomb had a time fuse that would automatically detonate it if the Air Force didn't find it and disarm it in time. There were all sorts of wild reports about what time the fuse was set for, but the story most generally believed was that the Air Force was keeping the time a secret in order to prevent panic.

By mid-morning it was hard to tell whether there were more people leaving town than were coming into it. The roads were clogged with traffic, and there were Air Force vehicles and brass all over the place. Reporters and TV camera crews kept showing up at the Town Hall, and by noontime every hotel room in town had been taken. The first question that nearly everybody asked was whether the water was safe to drink. It was almost impossible to make a telephone call out of town, because all the trunk lines were jammed with calls coming in.

Jeff and Harmon and I were sitting on the step in front of Snodgrass' Hardware Store, lagging pennies toward the edge of the curb and trying to figure out what we should do next, when Homer Snodgrass came out of the store munching an apple.

"Hi!" said Homer.

"Hi!" we said.

"Whatcha doin'?"

Harmon looked at him contemptuously. "Obviously, we're trying to fix this ice cream mixer so's we can have some ice cream."

"I don't see no ice cream mixer," said Homer, gnawing at the core of his apple.

"Well! You do have eyes, after all!" Harmon sneered. "I don't see no ice cream mixer, either. These here are pennies—which you probably don't recognize because you're always dealing with high finance in your dad's store—and we're trying to see who can lose his first."

"Very funny! How'd you like the rest of my apple?" Homer said, dangling the scraggly core in front of Harmon's face.

Harmon slapped at the apple core and it flew out into the street, where sparrows immediately descended upon it. Then he blew on the penny he was holding between his fingers, and pitched it out toward the curb. It landed flat on its side and skidded to within three inches of the edge. Harmon blew on his fingernails and polished them ostentatiously on his shirtfront.

"Sit down, Homer," he said politely. "Maybe I can give you a few lessons."

"Naw," said Homer. "My old man don't like guys sitting on the step."

"You want us to move?" Jeff asked him.

"Naw," said Homer. "It's just my old man don't like it."

"Somebody complaining?" Harmon asked.

"Just the customers," Homer replied. "Hey! I seen your picture in the paper this morning!"

Harmon was busy polishing his fingernails on his shirtfront again. "Yeah!" he yawned. "I had some important information for them. Trouble is, nobody will believe us."

"All kiddin' aside. You guys really know where that bomb is?"

"We think we do," Jeff explained, "but nobody will listen to us." Then he told Homer all about our fishing expedition, and the thing we heard drop in the water, and how we got kicked off the lake by the police. "They won't let anybody near the lake, so we can't find out whether there's really anything down there, or not. But it seems like it must have been the bomb."

"Yeah!" I agreed. "The Air Force didn't mention losing anything else."

"Hm-m," Homer pondered, as he settled his skinny frame onto the step beside us. "This may sound corny, but you've got a problem."

"Yeah!"

"What you need is a problem-solver."

"Right!"

"I know the best one in town."

"Who's that?"

"Henry Mulligan. He's the smartest kid I know."

"Oh, he ain't so smart!" sneered Harmon. "He just reads a lot."

Homer turned around slowly and glared at Harmon.

"At least he can read!"

A lot of kids don't like Henry Mulligan. They think he's a smart aleck, because he always has his homework done, and that makes the rest of us look bad. But the fact is, homework just comes easy to Henry, like a lot of other things do.

Jeff considered Homer's suggestion for a moment. But only for a moment. "Boy, I think you've hit it right on the button," he said. "Why didn't I think of that. If anybody can help us out, it's Henry Mulligan. Let's go talk to him."

"Henry's kinda far out," said Homer. "You gotta catch him in the right mood."

"That's true, if you're talking about fishing," said Jeff. "But if you've got a problem that has anything to do with...you know science and all that kinda stuff, boy, Henry is old Ready Teddy and rarin' to go. C'mon, let's get movin'.''

Jeff dashed to the curb, where his bike was leaning against a street light pole, and Harmon and I instinctively jumped up to follow him. Homer stayed behind on the step, scratching his mop of red hair.

"Hey!" he hollered. "My old man won't let me off 'til twelve-thirty."

"Meet us up at my barn!" Jeff cried, as he spun his bike around to head up Walnut Street. "We'll be there in half-an-hour, and Henry'll be with us."

"What about this three cents you left on the curb?" he shouted.

"That's for the birds!" Harmon shouted back. "But if there's any Indian heads, save 'em."

Henry Mulligan *was* with us when Homer showed up at Jeff Crocker's barn about an hour later, puffing like a blowfish, and mopping the sweat off his freckled face with a red bandanna handkerchief. We were in what used to be the tack room when Jeff's father had a lot of riding horses; but now it was just a musty old place where Jeff kept all his fishing gear, and his ham radio outfit, and just about everything else his mother wouldn't let him keep in the house.

"Look," he said, when he let Homer in the door, "we decided to use this as a meeting place until this business is all over, so if you're gonna join up with us, you gotta take the oath and then I'll tell you the secret knock that'll let you in. Otherwise, nobody gets in the door."

"Count me in!" Homer gasped. "I ain't peddlin' back to town 'til I've had a chance to rest up a bit."

"You're in!" said Jeff, slamming the door shut.

Homer stood there rubbing his eyes to adjust to the dim light of the tack room. "Where's Henry?" he asked.

"Here I am!" came a squeaky voice from the shadows in a dark corner of the room. Henry Mulligan sat there, propped on an old piano stool he had dug out from under a pile of old furniture and rugs stacked against one wall of the tack room. He had tilted back until his head and shoulders nestled comfortably in the angle of the walls, and had hooked his feet under the front legs of the stool to hold himself in suspension with only the rear legs of the stool in contact with the floor. His arms were crossed over his chest, and his glasses were pushed up onto his forehead, while his eyes stared blankly up at the cobwebs festooning the rafters of the barn.

"He's thinking," said Jeff. "Don't bother him."

"I can practically hear it," Homer murmured, as he

dusted off a box with his bandanna and sat down near the door.

"How long has he been like that, Charlie?" he whispered to me. I held up one hand and snapped all five fingers out twice, and Homer nodded. We all just sat there, while Henry thought and Harmon practiced some of his favorite mumbletypeg shots on the barn floor. Every time he missed, and the knife clattered on the floor, Henry's body would twitch, and Jeff would glare at Harmon. We all jumped when Henry asked a question without even moving his eyes.

"Can we get a good map of Strawberry Lake?"

"My dad's got all kinds of maps from the county engineers," said Jeff.

"Get one," said Henry, without moving.

When Jeff returned with a huge map tucked under his arm, Henry let his piano stool fall forward and adjusted his glasses over his eyes. We suspended an old door between two packing crates and spread the map out on it. Henry asked Jeff to point out the spot on the shore of the lake where we landed in the fog after hearing the bomb splash into the water. Then he sent him back to the house again for a protractor, ruler, and pencils.

"I think we can narrow this down pretty well, from what you've told me," he said as he started drawing lines on the map, "and then I have an idea how we can pinpoint the location of the bomb, if you want to."

"*If* we want to?" said Harmon. "What do you think we brought you all the way up here for?"

"Apple pie!" said Henry.

Harmon looked at Jeff, and Jeff threw his hands in the air and darted out the door again and into his mother's kitchen. He came back with two pieces of apple pie on a plate that still smelled warm, and we could hear Jeff's mother hollering at him from the kitchen window. We sat there with our mouths watering while Henry stuffed apple pie into his mouth and tried to explain what he was doing. He drew a line across the lake and asked Jeff if he agreed it represented the approximate line of flight of the bombers taking off from Westport Field. Jeff traced the line with his finger and nodded assent. Then Henry drew a line parallel to the North indicator on the map and plotted a line at 225 degrees from the point on the shore where we had landed in the fog. Where the line intersected with the flight path of the bombers he placed an "X".

"How far would you estimate you rowed to get back to shore?" he asked.

"Harmon counted four hundred eighty-five and-a-half strokes," said Jeff. "Forget the half."

"I will," said Henry. "It's not important. Let's see." Henry made some calculations on a piece of paper, then measured along the line we had taken with the rowboat. "If we estimate that four hundred and eighty-five strokes would take you about four thousand feet, that would put your position about here when you started for shore." He placed another "X" a little to the left of the line representing the flight path.

"That seems about right," said Jeff.

"Then I think we're close enough to know we're on the right track," Henry stated, drawing a rectangle along the flight path that enclosed the two Xs. "We'll search this area first, and if we don't find anything, we'll extend the search area out to here," and Henry drew a larger rectangle outside the first one.

"What are you talking about?" Harmon exclaimed.

"The Air Force won't even let us on the lake."

"We'll do it at night," Henry said, quietly, "when nobody can see us. The Air Force may have the lake off limits, but they can't possibly patrol the whole shore twenty-four hours a day."

"How can we see anything at night?" Homer asked.

"We don't have to see anything," Henry explained. "We'll use radio beacons from the shore to find our position."

"Okay! But how do we find the bomb?"

"Do you know what a magnetometer is?" Henry asked.

Everybody looked blank—especially Homer.

"A magnetometer is an instrument that measures the strength and the direction of the flux lines of the earth's magnetic field," Henry continued matter-of-factly while he went on plotting lines on the map. "Any metal object that has magnetic properties—especially steel and iron—will create a disturbance in the regular pattern of the magnetic flux lines surrounding the earth. The magnetometer can detect these disturbances; so all you do is move it over an area, and when it tells you something's wrong, you know there has to be some kind of metal there."

"You mean it's like a mine detector?" Homer asked.

"Sort of," said Henry, "but it's not the same thing at all. A mine detector sends out signals, and when it gets a good strong signal bouncing back, it usually means there's some kind of metal there. But it won't work for any great distance—you know, maybe a few feet under the ground. The magnetometer does the same job, but it doesn't send out any signals. It just senses the magnetic field and tells you if something is disturbing it. You can fly one in an airplane, two or three thousand feet in the air, and discover iron deposits 'way beneath the surface."

"Wow!" said Homer.

"Will it work over water?" Jeff asked.

"That's a good question!" said Henry, stuffing the last piece of apple pie into his mouth. "Shows you're thinking. Fact is, it takes a special kind of magnetometer to detect things under water. You have to tow it behind a boat on a line, but that's no problem."

"This is all very interesting, Mr. Genius," Harmon interrupted, "but I didn't happen to bring my magna...whatever-you-call-it...with me, and I'll bet nobody else did, so what good does that do us?"

Henry looked at Harmon as if he were some kind of a worm. "It happens that I know where I can borrow one," he said, "and if Jeff can get his mother to drive us over to the Lake & River Salvage Company in Claiborne, I know I can get Mr. Henderson to lend us one."

"Okay, okay!" said Harmon. "But it looks to me like we got a bigger job than we can handle. You gotta have at least two radio beacons at different places on shore to get a good fix on your position, and...."

"There are five of us," said Jeff, counting noses. "How many do we need in the boat, Henry?"

"Well, somebody has to row, 'cause we can't use your outboard motor—it would make too much noise. Then somebody's got to watch the indicator on the magnetometer, and somebody else has to keep us on course with a directional receiver...I guess we really ought to have two receivers...I've got one we can use, and you have one here...well, maybe we could do it with one, but it'll slow us up. I don't know. Now that you mention it, we're gonna be as busy as a dog act in a flea circus, but we'll manage somehow."

"We don't have to leave anybody with the beacon transmitters," Jeff suggested. "We can just set 'em out on the shore and turn 'em on."

"We could," Henry agreed, "but it would take a lot of time for us to set them up where we want them, and then get out on the lake with the boat. Besides, it isn't dark for too long this time of year. They've got to be pretty far apart, and roughly at right angles to each other." He indicated two points on the map where he thought we should place the beacon transmitters. One was on the north shore of the lake, almost due north of the area where we thought the bomb might be, and the other point was about where we estimated the flight path of the bombers crossed the shoreline.

"I know where we'll put that one," Jeff said. "Our lake cottage is right about there, and I know the bombers fly right over it whenever there's a scramble."

"Good!" said Henry. "We'll put Harmon there with one of the beacons and a walkie-talkie, and he can keep an eye on the police patrols in that area and let us know if they get the wind up."

"What if they send the police launch out after you?"

Henry scratched the thick hair over his right ear. "That's a good thought, Harmon. Some foxy old general once said that you never plan an attack without planning a line of retreat, and that's exactly what we've got to do. We'll take the outboard motor with us, Jeff, in case we have to use it."

"Okay! Now who does what?" Harmon interrupted. "We only got a few hours to get ready."

Henry scratched the hair over his right ear again,

and then jotted some notes on the margin of the map. "I guess we will need somebody else," he said. "I figure we ought to have four men in the boat to do this right. Anybody got any ideas?"

"What about Mortimer Dalrymple?" I suggested. "He's an old radio ham, like Jeff, and I know he's got a lot of equipment."

"Yeah! He's a regular electronic bug," Homer agreed. "But you got to get him excited about what you're doing, or he won't be interested. He's funny that way."

"I guess that lets him out," sneered Harmon. "I don't see how we can get him excited about looking for an atom bomb in a big lake in the middle of the night with the police and half the Air Force breathing down our necks. Better save him 'til we have something really hot going."

A lot of guys would have thrown a rabbit punch at Harmon for that one, but Homer isn't big on rabbit punches. He just looked sheepish, and his Adam's apple slid up and down his throat as he gulped, and his ears got a little red. "Okay, Okay," he said. "I'll go talk to Mortimer. Maybe he'll help us out."

"Maybe nothin'," Harmon replied. "I'll go with you. C'mon!" And he grabbed Homer by one of his red ears and propelled him through the door of the tack room.

Henry spent some more time calculating azimuths from the two radio beacon locations on the shoreline to various points on the two rectangles he had drawn in the lake, and entered the readings on dotted lines running from the rectangles to the shore. Then he handed the map to me.

"Charlie, you're in charge of the map, and that also

makes you the navigator," he said. "You've got to be able to tell us where we are, and how to get to where we want to go. Can you do it?"

I gulped once before I answered. "Sure! I guess I can."

"Good. Now bring a hooded flashlight along with you, and a board you can spread the map on in the bottom of the boat. We can't risk anybody seeing us from shore."

"Okay," I said, not really knowing what I was letting myself in for.

That night, Jeff and Harmon sneaked into Jeff's beach cottage and set up one of the beacon transmitters in an upstairs bedroom. Then they slipped the rowboat out of the boathouse, and Jeff rowed it quietly up the shore toward Turkey Hill Road, leaving Harmon behind to man the transmitter. Henry and I were waiting for him there with Mortimer Dalrymple. We had hidden our bicycles in the brush back of the beach.

Henry had sent Homer off with the other beacon transmitter with instructions to set it up at a cove on the north shore of the lake where we knew there was an elevation marker put there by the U. S. Coast and Geodetic Survey. Elevation markers are called bench marks. They're little square pillars of concrete sunk in the ground to mark points where the altitude above sea level has been measured very precisely. Henry picked the spot because the location of these markers is also known very precisely, and all topographical maps are based on them. With this as a basic reference point, we had a much better chance of knowing exactly where we were on the lake if we located anything, and we could pinpoint it on the map.

As soon as Jeff had beached the boat we started

loading our equipment into it, and my spine started tingling as I realized we were actually going to do what we had been talking about most of the day.

"Hurry up!" Jeff said in a tense voice. "A police patrol might come along the road any minute and see us here."

No sooner had he said it than a beam of light flashed by us and briefly illuminated the beach. But it came from the lake, not the road.

"Hit the dirt!" Mortimer Dalrymple cried, throwing himself behind a huge boulder with his receiver and loop antenna cradled in his arms.

"Help me with the boat! Help me with the boat!" Jeff hissed in a hoarse whisper.

Henry and I ran to the water's edge and shoved and tugged with Jeff 'til we got the boat into a patch of tall reeds at the edge of the beach. We flopped into it just as the light swept past us again, probed back and forth for a few seconds, then passed on up the shore of the lake. Jeff's walkie-talkie, slung over his shoulder, started crackling. Jeff ran the antenna up and spoke into the mouthpiece. "Jeff here."

"This is Harmon. There's a patrol boat out on the lake. Better watch it."

"Have you got any other news?" Jeff cracked. "How about giving us more notice next time?"

"Sorry about that," said Harmon, "but I just saw the light."

"Let's get out of here," Jeff panted, all out of breath. "Let's call it off, Henry."

"Calm down," Henry advised him, matter-of-factly. "They've got to circle the whole lake before they get back here again. Once we get out on the lake, they're not likely to see us. They're searching the shoreline, which is what they have to do. The best time to get out there is right now."

"You always have it figured out," said Jeff, grudgingly. And he started pushing the boat out of the reeds.

About ten minutes later we were out on the lake jockeying the boat into position so Mortimer and I could get the right azimuth readings to the two beacon transmitters. We had wrapped the oarlocks in burlap to cut down noise, and kept the receivers on very low volume. We could see a patrol boat sweeping the shoreline with its searchlight, but it was seldom any closer than about a mile from us. Obviously, they didn't really expect anybody to be out on the lake, and were just taking the precaution of patrolling the shoreline. After two sweeps around the lake, the boat confined its activities to just searching the beachfront on the Mammoth Falls side of the lake.

We stayed out there about an hour and a half, with Jeff rowing us back and forth in what we figured was the area of the smaller rectangle Henry had drawn on the map. The magnetometer was swimming along behind us on the end of a towline, and Henry was crouched in the stern seat, using a pencil flashlight to scan the readout on the oscillograph. Once in awhile he would hold his hand up and tell Jeff to stop. Then we would back up a bit and go over the same spot again until Henry was satisfied there was nothing significant showing on the graph. It was a bit sticky trying to keep Jeff on an even course; but it wasn't too important as long as we knew approximately where we were. If Henry found something startling, there would be time enough to figure out our exact position.

We were just a few hundred yards off the head of a heavily-wooded peninsula that juts far out into the lake from the northeast shore, when Henry let out a *"Whoop!"* that almost made us jump out of our skins. You know how it is when everybody is trying to be quiet, and somebody suddenly corks off with a loud shout. It really startles you. Jeff was just giving a hefty tug on the oars when Henry shouted, and he fell flat on his back as one oar slipped out of the oarlock and clattered into the boat.

"Back up! Back up!" Henry shouted again.

"Anything you say, Maestro," Jeff retorted, "but do you have to be so dramatic about it?"

"Whatever it is, I think it'll stay there," came Mortimer's steady voice from the bow. "I'd suggest we sneak up on it quietly, so we don't attract any unnecessary attention."

Jeff gathered himself together and started pushing on the oars to get us back to the spot where Henry had apparently gotten an unusual reading on the oscillograph. Henry reeled in the magnetometer and held it at the stern of the boat until we were far enough back. Then he let out the tow line again.

"Now, go slow," he cautioned Jeff. "And if I hold my hand up, back water a bit, 'til I tell you to go ahead."

We retraced our original route again, and sure enough, Henry held his hand up and we all held our breath. Then he motioned Jeff forward a bit and held his hand up again.

"There's something here, all right!" he whispered excitedly. "Try to hold her still, Jeff, while I get a good reading to the two beacons."

Mortimer and I tuned our receivers as close as we

could, and adjusted the loop antennas until we got the highest amplitude signal from the beacons. Mortimer read 350 degrees to the transmitter that Homer had taken to the bench mark on the north shore of the lake, and I measured about 100 degrees back to Jeff's beach cottage where Harmon was sending out the signal. I noted both the readings on the margin of the map, and asked Henry, "What do we do now?"

"We've done all we can tonight," Henry answered, as he reeled in the magnetometer. "I'd suggest we get out of here."

No sooner had he said it, than the big searchlight from the patrol boat swept past us. We had been so busy we hadn't noticed it working its way toward our end of the lake. We all ducked instinctively, but there wasn't much point in it. The light came back from the other direction, passed us once more, then flicked back and caught us in the dead center of its beam. A loud voice from a bullhorn came blasting across the water at us, but we couldn't make out the words.

"Tell 'em we're just fishing!" Mortimer snorted.

"It may not be all that funny," Jeff retorted, as he pulled the oars into the boat. "Let's get that outboard motor started, Henry."

Henry was all thumbs, trying to get the magnetometer equipment stowed safely on the bottom of the boat, and at the same time make room for Jeff to get the motor started. We could hear the motors of the patrol boat churn as the craft started to pick up speed, heading straight for us.

"What's all the fuss about?" Mortimer persisted. "All they can do is tell us to get off the lake."

"Yeah? And then ask what we're doing out here with

all this radio equipment and stuff like that."

"So, they put us in jail for the night. At least we'd get a free breakfast."

"I just don't want to get caught!" Jeff shouted, as the outboard motor sputtered, coughed, and then started to purr like a kitten.

"Head for the north shore of that peninsula," Henry cried, waving a free arm in that direction. "There's plenty of coves we can hide in where they'll never find us."

"*If* we get there in time!" Jeff flung back at him, as he threw the motor into a right-hand turn.

From then on it was a race, with the patrol boat gaining on us as we rounded the head of the peninsula and slipped into the shadow of its trees and craggy rocks. With no moon out we were in pitch darkness again, and Jeff had to throttle down until he could make out the dim outline of the shore. We could hear the siren of the patrol boat, and the voice still hollering through the bull horn.

"Turn it on, Jeff, they're gaining on us!" Henry panted.

"I can't see where I'm going," Jeff complained. "Hand me a flashlight."

I fumbled around in the bottom of the boat and came up with one that I passed to him. At the same time Mortimer flicked on his own high-powered torch and trained it on the shoreline. The north shore of the peninsula we were skirting is steep and rocky. It is a tangle of tree roots, huge boulders, and fallen tree trunks at the water's edge; and in some places there are sheer granite walls, twenty or thirty feet high, rising straight up to the tree line. And some distance out from the shore there are solid pinnacles of granite jutting

just as high out of the water. It's one of the most pic-
turesque parts of the lakeshore in the daytime, but not
quite the place to be at night with nothing but starlight
to see by.

Jeff was keeping far enough out to avoid the rocks,
but we had to get in closer to shore and find a place to
hide before the patrol boat made its way around the
head of the peninsula.

"There's a good place!" shouted Mortimer, who was
probing the shoreline ahead of us with his high-powered beam. He trained his light on a narrow slip of
water between two huge masses of rock about two hundred feet ahead of us.

"I hope we can get the boat through there," Jeff
answered, "but we don't have time to be choosy.
Charlie, get ready to take over with the oars when I
throttle down."

I grabbed one of the oars and Henry grabbed the
other, and we propped them on the gunwales. The two
massive pinnacles of granite were fairly close in to the
shore, and it was possible there was a small cove in
behind them. But even if there wasn't, the rocks might
give us enough concealment to escape the probing light
of the patrol boat. It was the only chance we had. The
engines of the patrol boat were growing louder, and we
could already sense the darkness being dissipated by its
powerful light as it drew closer to the head of the
peninsula.

Jeff charged at the opening between the rocks with
the throttle wide open, as Mortimer kept his light
trained on it. About twenty feet from it he threw the
motor into reverse, and the boat wallowed low in the
water until he cut the power off. Then we slipped forward

silently, and Henry and I paddled frantically to nose the boat into the narrow crevice between the rocks. When we were in it, we all reached out and clawed the face of the rocks to pull the boat in out of sight.

But there was no cove! We slipped out from between the two rocks and into open water again.

"Back it up! Back it up!" Mortimer shouted, and we all frantically paddled water with our hands until we got the boat back in between the two rocks. We bobbed up and down there, clinging to the back of the outermost rock with our hands, and pressing our bodies close up to it. The light of the patrol boat suddenly turned the darkness into daylight, but the shadow of the rock covered us—almost. It was easy to see that once the patrol boat had passed us, the prow of our boat would be sticking out in plain view beyond the other side of the rock. If they flashed their light back as they went by, they'd get a good view of the nose of our boat and Mortimer's bare face hanging out.

Jeff sensed the situation first. "When I give the signal, push to your left," he cried. "We've got to get the boat around to the other side of the rock!"

We all braced hard against the rock, holding our breath as the patrol boat churned by us. It was going very slowly now, picking its way carefully along the shore. It seemed to take forever, and its searchlight was raking back and forth among the rocks very deliberately.

"Push! Push!" Mortimer suddenly shouted, pressing hard against the rock face and not waiting for Jeff's signal. "They've got the light on me."

I glanced to my right and saw Mortimer silhouetted against the bright beam of the searchlight. Instinctively, I started to shove against the gritty surface of the rock and found nothing there. My hands flailed helplessly in front of me, and I could feel the boat slipping out from beneath my feet. The next thing I knew, I hit the water in a spectacular belly-whopper and went under heels up.

You know how it is when you hit the water unexpectedly. You always seem to be taking a breath at the time you go under, and you come up sputtering water in all directions and seeing stars before your eyes. My nose was chock-full of Strawberry Lake when I got back up to the surface, and I shook my head and struck out for the nearest thing I could see. It was the granite wall of the rock we had been hiding behind. I clung to it, and looked around for the others. One by one they came bobbing up and scrambled for a handhold on one or the other of the two rocks. The light of the patrol boat flashed by us once more, but harmlessly. We were all safe in the shadow of the rocks, and we clung there until the sound of the boat's engines faded into the distance. Then Mortimer's strident voice broke the momentary silence.

"Hey! Has anybody got a cake of soap? Might as well have a real bath while we're at it."

"Cut the comedy!" Jeff sputtered, coughing up lake water. "Get the boat. They may be back here any minute."

He was right. Mortimer and I sprang out from the rock and corralled the rowboat before it drifted away from us. We pulled it back between the rocks, and sure enough the patrol boat circled back to take another look. We all stayed in the water, maneuvering the rowboat into the shadow of the outer rock as the light probed back and forth around us.

Finally the patrol boat churned away on its search for the phantom rowboat it thought it had seen, and we pulled for the shore, tugging our boat behind us. We crawled up on a narrow strip of beach and flopped down in the sand to get our breath.

"I can think of better ways to spend an evening," Henry Mulligan gasped as he wrung the water out of his jeans. "Did any of our equipment get wet?"

"Before we worry about that, let's get this boat out of sight," said Jeff. "We're not out of it yet."

"How are we gonna get back home?" Mortimer asked.

"On our feet!" Jeff replied. "We can either follow the shore back, which is the long way, or we can cut over the ridge to Turkey Hill Road and walk back to where you guys stashed your bikes. We'll have to hide the boat somewhere, and what we can't carry with us we'll have to leave here and come back and get it tomorrow night."

Then Jeff got on the radio and told Harmon and Homer to knock it off for the night, and meet us in the morning at his barn. We snooped along the shoreline until we found a little cove where we could pull the boat in out of sight among the rocks and bushes, and we covered it with the tarpaulin and left most of our equipment in it. We took the map and the magnetometer with us, and whatever else we could carry. We had to scale the cliff of the peninsula and make our way through some pretty rough woods strewn with boulders before we even got to the mainland, where we had to clamber over the ridge of hills between the lake and Turkey Hill Road. After all the excitement we'd had, I thought we'd never make it. But we did finally reach the hard surface of the road, and I was glad to see Homer come pedaling along on his way back home. I volunteered to ride down the road with him and bring back two of our bicycles, and that saved us a little time. As it was, I didn't get home until nearly midnight and had a long, involved argument with my mother about where I'd been and why I couldn't get home earlier. But, when I finally got to bed I felt pretty good. I stretched out between the sheets and fell to sleep in no time, with the feeling that we had really accomplished something that night. Somehow or other, I felt sure we had discovered the location of the bomb.

But we soon found out it wasn't so easy convincing other people.

The Frustration
of Henry Mulligan

The next morning we all met at Jeff's barn to decide
what to do next. Henry very carefully drew on the map
the azimuth readings we had measured to the two beacon transmitters, and he marked a tight red circle
where they intersected.

"I think if we take this down to the Town Hall and
show it to Mayor Scragg, he might convince the Air
Force to send divers down there and take a look,"
Henry said.

"And if they find the bomb there, that ought to make
us look like heroes," said Mortimer Dalrymple.

"Yeah! Just like it did the last time," Harmon
Muldoon grunted. "All I got was a pat on the head and
a busted toe."

"Too bad it wasn't the other way around," Mortimer observed. "I'm in favor of doing just what Henry says."

We took a vote and decided the best thing to do was to go right to the Town Hall with our information, even though Harmon Muldoon argued loudly for going down to the Mammoth Falls *Gazette* office and telling them everything we knew. As things turned out, we probably should have listened to Harmon.

To begin with, it was almost impossible to see Mayor Scragg or anyone else of any importance. Both the Town Hall and the town square were crawling with people we'd never seen before, and the automobile traffic around the place was something you wouldn't believe. There were state cars, and county cars, and cars from the Department of Agriculture, and the Air Force, and the Red Cross, and you name it. Air Police from Westport Field were helping to direct traffic, because Chief Putney just didn't have enough men to handle the job.

In front of the Town Hall there was a white-haired old character wearing sandals and a flowing white robe walking up and down with a sign that said: REPENT BEFORE THE BOMB GOES OFF! News photographers and a couple of TV crews were shooting pictures of him. And, as usual, there was a raggle-taggle bunch of kids and stray dogs parading along behind him. Every time they got in front of the photographers the kids would stick their thumbs in their ears and wiggle their fingers at the cameras and the dogs would lift their noses in the air and howl. I don't know when I've seen so much excitement in the square except for the day, later on, when we flew a life-sized mannequin off the top of Hannah Kimball's statue and broke up the

Founder's Day ceremony.

Things were booming in Mammoth Falls, despite the fact a lot of people had left town out of sheer panic. For every person who had left town, though, it seemed that two more had come in either because they had a job to do, or because they saw a chance to capitalize on the situation. A good example was Seth Hawkins. And we soon discovered he was the principal reason we couldn't get to see Mayor Scragg, or anybody else in authority.

Seth Hawkins has been the congressman for Mammoth Falls for thirty-seven years, and he's never had his picture in any newspaper except the Mammoth Falls *Gazette* and the Claiborne *Times* since he first went to Washington. Now, with Mammoth Falls the center of national attention, Seth was Johnny-on-the-spot at the scene of action, and he had already announced he would hold a press conference as soon as he had conferred with Mayor Scragg and Colonel March.

We wandered around in the Town Hall, following Henry as he went from one person to another trying to find someone who would listen to him. No matter whom he talked to they all said the same thing: "That's very interesting, Sonny. Why don't you show that map to Colonel March?" But Colonel March was locked in conference with Mayor Scragg and Congressman Hawkins, and nobody could get to him.

"Nuts to this!" said Harmon Muldoon, finally. And he snatched the map out of Henry's hand and stalked out the front door of the Town Hall with it, heading straight for the TV crews lounging under the elm trees.

Henry stood there with his mouth open, but Jeff and I took off after Harmon. He marched straight down the steps and across the street, waving the map in the air and shouting, "Hey, you guys! You wanna know where that bomb is? It's right here."

A cluster of reporters and cameramen gathered around him while Harmon blurted out the story of what the lines and circles on the map meant.

"Where'd you get this map, kid?" one of the reporters asked.

"It's *our* map!" Harmon answered, truculently.

"Well, who put all these marks on it? How do you know that's where the bomb is?"

"*We* did," said Harmon. "We were up all night dragging a magnometer all over the lake so we could find the bomb."

"What's a *magnometer*?" asked another reporter.

"That's a mag-ne-*tom*eter," said Jeff, quietly.

"Yeah, that's a mag-ne-*tom*eter, stupid," said Harmon. "Don't you guys know nothin' about science?"

By that time, Henry had joined us and Jeff pushed him into the center of the group. Then he elbowed Harmon into the background while Henry quietly explained to the reporters what the map was all about. One of them, a big raw-boned man with a shock of red hair and freckles, took a special interest in the map.

"Is this on the level?" he asked Henry. "Did you kids really go out on that lake? What about the radiation?"

"Oh, pooh!" said Henry. "What was the police launch doing out there? If there was any radiation they wouldn't be out there either."

"You're right. I never thought of that."

"C'mon, Jenkins," one of the other reporters grumbled. "These kids don't know what they're talking about. Just 'cause they got a map with a bunch of marks on it don't mean they know where that bomb is."

"I'm not so sure," said Jenkins.

"Don't be nuts," said a little man with a camera. "We got a story to cover. You start messing around with these kids, and we'll miss it if something big happens."

"What do you mean, something big? I don't see the Air Force doin' anything," said Jenkins. "Maybe a story about some kids who think they know where the bomb fell is the only story we'll get today."

"Suit yourself," said the cameraman. "But I think you're a sucker. These kids are pulling your leg."

"Wait a minute, Mr. Jenkins," said Jeff, stepping forward. "We're not pulling anybody's leg. We're telling the truth, and we can't get anybody to listen to us. I was out there on the lake when the bomb dropped, and we know where it is—at least, we *think* it was the bomb."

The uncertainty in Jeff's voice at this point brought some chuckles and a few wisecracks from the group of reporters. The little cameraman shrugged his shoulders as if to say, "I told you so!" and shuffled off into the shade of the tree where his equipment was. In a moment he was back.

"Hey, look, Jenkins! Look what's comin' up the street!" the little cameraman yelled. "Hey, I gotta get this on film! Maybe we got a story for the early news. Look at that, will ya. Look at it!" And he dashed back to grab his camera.

We all looked in the direction he was gesturing; and there, coming up Vesey Street, was a column of black umbrellas that reached from curb to curb and stretched out of sight around a bend. At the head of the column marched Abigail Larrabee, president of the Greater Mammoth Falls Garden Circle, and also president of the Mammoth Falls chapter of the Friends of the Wildwood. High over her head she brandished her umbrella with the words "MARCH ON MARCH!" painted on it. Right behind her strode a ponderous woman proudly holding aloft a huge beach umbrella that had been dyed black, and on it were painted the words, "NO FISSION ALLOWED IN STRAWBERRY LAKE!" Other umbrellas carried sayings like, "FIND THE BOMB NOW!", "GET THE JET SET OUT OF TOWN!", and "BOMB IS A FOUR-LETTER WORD!"

People were pouring out of stores and offices along Vesey Street to watch the parade. Some of them were laughing at the signs, and a lot of the men were making uncomplimentary cat-calls. But most of the onlookers started clapping their hands in time to the cadence of the marchers. Mrs. Larrabee acknowledged the applause with gracious nods of her head from side to side as she proceeded up the street. But the large woman behind her plodded steadfastly along with her eyes fixed on the clock tower of the Town Hall. The women streaming along behind were mostly solemn-faced and angry, but some of them were also embarrassed at being the center of attention and were blushing and giggling at the cat-calls from the men.

When they reached the corner where Vesey Street dead-ends at the Town Hall, a battery of photographers and reporters met them. But the women marched straight on without breaking stride, and the members of the press tagged along, pumping questions and snapping pictures. The little TV cameraman with Mr. Jenkins was walking backwards in front of Mrs. Larrabee, shooting a close-up of her face. When he stopped momentarily to rewind his camera, Mrs. Larrabee brushed right past

him and he stumbled into the path of the female behe-
moth following her, who bowled him over like a ten pin.
He went down in a tangle of arms and legs, with his
camera skidding across the pavement, and the first four
ranks of the column of marching umbrellas tromped
right over him.

Right around the square the procession wheeled,
and then drew up in a tight semicircle before the steps
of the Town Hall. The women raised their umbrellas
on high and started screaming out the slogans painted
on them. Mrs. Larrabee, flanked by three women on
either side, started up the Town Hall steps with the
ponderous woman with the beach umbrella puffing
right behind her.

"C'mon!" cried Jeff. "Let's get a good seat so we can
watch the fun."

We dashed through the crowd of onlookers milling
in the street and clambered up the trees that border
the walk in front of the Town Hall. Mrs. Larrabee had
just reached the top of the steps when I settled myself
in a crotch of one of the maples. She was immediately
confronted by Constable Billy Dahr, whose moustache
was bobbing up and down in rhythm with the billy club
he waggled back and forth behind his back. On either
side of him stood an Air Policeman at parade rest.

"What are you doing here, Mr. Dahr?" asked Mrs.
Larrabee in her most imperious tone.

"I'm on duty, Ma'am," said Billy Dahr, turning to one
side to squirt a stream of tobacco juice between the polished boots of one of the Air Policemen. "The mayor's in
conference with Congressman Hawkins and Colonel
March, and nobody's allowed in 'til the meeting's over."

"Humph!" said Mrs. Larrabee.

"Humph!" said the huge woman behind her.

"Matilda!" Mrs. Larrabee sang out with a rising inflection as she stepped to one side.

"Follow me, Abigail!" cried the big woman, as she bulldozed her way right between Billy Dahr and one of the Air Policemen, knocking them both aside as though they had been stalks of straw.

Mrs. Larrabee did a right pivot as expertly as any quarterback following a blocking guard through a hole in the line, and disappeared in the dim shadows of the lobby of the Town Hall.

The women gathered at the foot of the Town Hall steps shrieked ecstatically and thrust their umbrellas into the air with cries of "Go get 'em, Matilda!" and "Atta girl, Abigail!" Matilda Pratt, the big woman with the beach umbrella, was a favorite of theirs and well known in Mammoth Falls for two reasons: the fact she weighs over three hundred pounds, and the fact she has thirteen children—all of them girls. At school, the teachers claim they can always recognize a new Pratt girl by the dress she's wearing. One teacher claims the same dress has been in her class for ten years, but there's always a different girl in it. One year, Lillian Pratt got held back in the fifth grade, and that caused a problem. The teacher didn't recognize Lillian in next year's dress, and every morning she'd send her into the sixth grade classroom, where she did pretty well for a couple of weeks until they got the matter straightened out.

Anyway, we all knew something would happen pretty soon; because, when a Pratt barges into a meeting, the meeting usually breaks up. The sheer bulk of her presence is enough to make the room seem crowded. And, sure enough, it wasn't long before Chief Putney came

out to the top of the steps and was greeted by shouts
and screams from the women, who pumped their
umbrellas up and down and chanted slogans when he
held up his hands for silence.

"Ladies! Ladies!" he shouted, at the top of his voice.
"Please be patient!"

"We want Mayor Scragg!" shouted several of the
women, crowding up the steps toward him.

"We want Colonel March!" shouted others, pushing
behind them.

Chief Putney didn't want to retreat, but what else
could he do? You just can't start pushing women around
in public. They backed Chief Putney right up to the
doors of the Town Hall, where he stood spread-eagled
against them, flanked by the two Air Policemen and
Constable Billy Dahr.

"Ladies, ladies!" he implored. "I just came out to tell
you that His Honor, the Mayor, and Colonel March will
be glad to come out and talk to you."

"He'd better come out, or he won't get any supper!"
snapped a tall, gaunt woman in the crowd.

"Oh! How do you do, Mrs. Scragg," said Chief
Putney, tipping his hat politely. "I didn't expect to see
you among this bunch of...er...this group of fine
ladies." Having already stepped in it, the chief had sim-
ply stuck his foot in further.

"Well! The very idea!" said Mrs. Scragg, drawing
herself up to full height.

"Another crack like that, and you won't get any supper!" said a short, stocky woman, pushing her way to
the front.

Chief Putney's mouth dropped open, then he glowered
at the woman. "What on earth are you doing here,

Penelope?"

"I came down to hear the speech."

"What speech? Nobody's giving a speech."

"*Somebody* will give a speech before we leave here, Harold. Now, you just nip inside and bring those nice gentlemen out here."

Chief Putney muttered something to himself and mashed his hat back onto his head. But he did as he was told and strode back into the Town Hall with the peculiar foot-swinging gait he affected when he was on official business. In less than a minute, Abigail Larrabee and Matilda Pratt came out through the doors and herded the women back down the steps, where they lined up in a tight formation with their umbrellas raised on high. They were followed almost immediately by Mayor Scragg, with Colonel March and Congressman Hawkins trailing behind him. Colonel March was the only one of the three who looked composed and at ease; and I figured this was because he didn't have to worry about whether anybody voted for him.

Mayor Scragg paused at the top of the steps and ran his finger around the inside of his collar. "It's very nice to see you all here today, ladies," he said. "I'm sure the other...."

"We want to know what you're doing about the bomb, Mr. Mayor!" said Abigail Larrabee matter-of-factly.

"Er...yes!" said the mayor. "Naturally...you want to know about the bomb. Well, I can say...."

"We know about the bomb. It's in the lake. We want to know what you're doing about it," she persisted.

"Ah...yes, indeed. Exactly!" said the mayor. "Well, the fact is, Mrs. Larrabee, we are not one-hundred-percent certain the bomb is in the lake. But I can assure you...."

"If it ain't in the lake, how come you can't find it?"
came the booming voice of Matilda Pratt.

Mayor Scragg winced noticeably. "First of all, ladies,
I want to assure that there is no danger. Colonel March
has assured me that...."

"How come all of my peonies have wilted?" asked
Mrs. Larrabee.

"Our chickens haven't laid any eggs for two days,"
said another woman.

"The water don't taste good," said another.

Then the cap sort of blew off the fizz bottle. The
women started shouting slogans and complaints, and
thrusting their umbrellas up in the air. Then they began
stamping their feet in rhythm, and pretty soon they were
milling around in a figure eight and shaking their fist at
the mayor every time they passed in front of him. Mayor
Scragg was holding his hands up for silence and trying to
say something, but nobody could hear him.

Then the strident voice of Abigail Larrabee cut
through the clamor. "We want *action*, Mr. Mayor, not
explanations!" she shouted.

"Please! Please! Ladies..." the mayor pleaded, pushing
the palms of his hands out toward them. "Please listen
to me!" But his voice was drowned in the uproar.
Complaint after complaint was flung at him.

"Our cow's milk was sour this morning!"

"My grass is turning brown!"

"My baby has broken out in a rash!—She never had
one before!"

"And we can't flush our toilet!" shouted Mortimer
Dalrymple at the top of his lungs.

Jeff Crocker gave him a vicious elbow in the ribs

that almost unseated Mortimer from his perch. "Shut up!" he said through clenched teeth.

"Well, how daffy can you get?" Mortimer complained. "These women are ridiculous."

"Okay! Okay!" said Jeff. "But they're doing all right. We gotta watch for a chance to grab the mayor and Colonel March."

While the women continued milling about and shouting their complaints, Mayor Scragg pleaded with Chief Putney to do something about the demonstration. But Chief Putney just shook his head.

"What do you want me to do, Mr. Mayor? Put them all in jail?"

"Well, there must be something you can do! You're the Chief of Police, aren't you?" the mayor shouted.

"Sure I am!" the chief shouted back. "But I haven't had any training in hitting women over the head!"

Meanwhile, a couple of TV cameramen had gotten up onto the steps and were having a regular heyday filming the proceedings. One of them kept waving at the women to get them to turn the signs on their umbrellas toward the cameras. Another man was holding a microphone on a long pole out over their heads and hollering at them to shout louder. Then the other cameraman handed one of the women a broken tree branch and said:

"Shake that at the mayor while we get a few shots, will you?"

Once they realized they were being photographed, the women tried to out do each other in thinking up spectacular things to do. A few of them got bold enough to stick their tongues out at the mayor; and two of them even cupped their fingers around their lips and tried to give the mayor a raspberry, which didn't come off too well because they hadn't had much practice in giving the good, ear-splitting kind that gets attention. There was a lot of jostling going on as everybody fought for a good position in front of the cameras.

Finally, Matilda Pratt came down off the steps and waded into the throng. She grabbed two of the women by the arms and gave them a good shaking. All of a sudden the hullabaloo stopped and the women settled down again in front of the steps.

Mayor Scragg cleared his throat and ran his finger around the inside of his collar once more. Then he caught sight of Mrs. Scragg in the crowd before him.

"Hello, dear!" he said with a nervous smile, wiggling his fingers in her direction.

"Speak up, Alonzo!" said Mrs. Scragg. "The ladies want to hear what you have to say."

"Er...yes...exactly..." said the mayor.

"Well?" said Abigail Larrabee.

"Perhaps it would be best if I just answered your questions," said the mayor. "Do you have any questions, ladies?"

There was a stony silence.

"*Somebody* must have a question," said the mayor.

"We've asked all our questions," came the booming voice of Matilda Pratt from under the beach umbrella. "We're waiting for answers, now!"

Mayor Scragg looked flustered; but, fortunately, a disturbance at the rear of the crowd attracted everyone's attention.

"I have a question, Mr. Mayor!" came a voice from behind the crowd.

There stood Mr. Jenkins, the red-headed TV reporter, brandishing our map of Strawberry Lake above his head. Henry Mulligan stood beside him; and when they started to move toward the Town Hall steps, Jeff Crocker shinnied down the maple tree across the sidewalk from me and caught up with them.

"I have a question for Colonel March," Jenkins said, in a voice loud enough for everyone to hear. "You said you weren't sure the bomb was in the lake, Mr. Mayor. And yesterday Colonel March said that divers were searching the lake thoroughly. I want to know, Colonel, whether your divers have searched this part of the lake?" And he pointed to the rectangles Henry had drawn on our map.

Colonel March studied the map carefully. "Ah yes!" he said. "I know that area. I received the report that some boys out fishing had heard something fall in the lake in that general vicinity—or thought they did. That was one of the first places we searched."

"You think maybe the boys didn't hear anything after all?"

"I don't know," the colonel replied. "You know, you get a lot of peculiar reports from all kinds of people in a situation like this. You have to follow up on most of them, of course, but a lot of them turn out to be pure imagination—or even deliberate pranks. All I know is that we have searched that part of the lake."

"Excuse me, sir!" came a squeaky voice from behind Mr. Jenkins. "What did you find there?"

The colonel looked a bit surprised as Henry Mulligan stepped out to confront him. "What do you mean?" he asked, looking from Henry to Mr. Jenkins.

"I want to know, sir, what you found when your divers searched that part of the lake."

"Well, nothing, obviously," said the colonel, with an

amused smile beginning to show on his face.

"Nothing? But they must have found *something*! There's something down there," Henry persisted.

"They found nothing," said the colonel, with a shrug. "And they searched the lake bottom very thoroughly. It's very deep in that area, you know."

"I know it is," said Henry. "But there's something there. And it's metallic. There's a big anomaly in that area."

"There's a big what?"

"A big anomaly, sir. It's almost got to be the bomb."

"I don't know what you're talking about, young man," said Colonel March, with a tolerant smile. "I can only say we have eliminated that area as a possibility."

At this point, Congressman Hawkins stepped forward rather obtrusively, as though he was afraid the meeting might break up before he had a chance to say anything. He thrust his hand out with the fingers spread wide apart, and with a toothy grin introduced himself to Mr. Jenkins.

"If you don't mind, sir, I should like to ask this young man a question."

"Ask him anything you like," said Mr. Jenkins. "He doesn't belong to me."

"Ah, yes! Well, young man, what was it you said you found out there in the lake?"

"We didn't exactly find anything, Mr. Hawkins," Henry answered. "But we did detect a definite magnetic anomaly, right about there on the map."

"Ah, yes! That's what I thought you had said. I just wanted to make sure."

"But I didn't exactly say that," said Henry. "All I said was we had found an anomaly."

"Oh, yes...yes! But any fool would know what you meant," said Seth Hawkins, patting Henry indulgently on the head. You could just about see the hair stand up on the back of Henry's neck. "You know, Mr. Jenkins, we who are native to this area know that Strawberry Lake is famous for its fish, and I take great pride in the fact that these young constituents of mine are showing some concern about the matter of this bomb and its possible effect...."

"Did you want to make a statement, Congressman?" Mr. Jenkins interrupted.

"I certainly do," said Mr. Hawkins, without pausing for breath. "And I want to make it perfectly clear that I, for one, do not intend to stand idly by and see...."

"I know the rest of that one!" said Mr. Jenkins. "If you don't mind, Mr. Congressman, I'd like to ask you a few questions over here in front of the camera."

"By all means, sir!" said Mr. Hawkins, obligingly doffing his hat and allowing himself to be escorted toward the corner of the Town Hall steps. The little cameraman had mounted his camera dolly there and a cluster of other reporters had already gathered. Henry had to go along, too, because the congressman had a firm grip on his shoulder and wouldn't let go. The crowd of women started streaming up the steps and practically surrounded the reporters, and Mayor Scragg and Colonel March got pushed back against the Town Hall doors.

All of a sudden Congressman Hawkins was the center of attention, and you could tell he knew it. He started talking long before the television crew could get ready, and Mr. Jenkins had to stop him twice.

"I'd like to ask you a few questions, if you'd just wait a minute, sir. We have to get a sound level, first." Then he stuck a microphone in front of the congressman's face. "Would you mind saying a few words, now."

"What do you want me to say?"

"Anything. Anything at all. We just want to get a voice level on you."

"Well...I don't know...Uh...I can't think of anything to say."

"That's fine!" said Mr. Jenkins, getting a signal from his sound man. "That's just fine; I think we're all set to go now."

By this time, Harmon and I had managed to crawl through the crowd of women on our hands and knees and squeeze into a spot on the base of one of the granite columns right behind Jeff and Mortimer. There was an air of excitement in the crowd, with everybody pushing in closer to hear what the congressman would have to say—or maybe to try and heckle him, and Harmon got a little carried away. He started jumping up and down with his thumbs in his ears, waggling his fingers at the TV camera. Then he stuck his chest out and made sweeping gestures with his right arm, as if was giving a speech; and pretty soon he was screwing his rubber face up into all sorts of contortions, and crossing his eyes, and making a general jackass of himself. It was too crowded to move away from him, so finally Jeff had to drive an elbow into his belly button and Harmon sort of collapsed against the granite column. Sometimes Harmon can be a problem.

Mr. Jenkins waggled the microphone in front of Congressman Hawkins' face, blew on it a few times, and then cleared his throat. "I'll start off with the big question, Mr. Congressman.... Do you feel there is any danger of this bomb going off?"

"That's a loaded question," said the congressman. "I

have no comment."

"What about the danger of radiation?"

"Well...uh...." Mr. Hawkins looked around at the faces of the women. "I think Colonel March has answered that question adequately...uh...."

There was a loud grumbling sound among the women, and Matilda Pratt started shaking the huge beach umbrella at the congressman.

"However...what I mean to say is...there are a great many factors that have to be considered," he continued, "and I am sure that these lovely ladies here have good reason for their complaints...and...harrruumph...and that their opinion has to be listened to, also."

There were cheers and cries of *"Hear! Hear!"* at this. Congressman Hawkins was shifting from one foot to the other and looking uncomfortable.

"You haven't answered my question!" said Mr. Jenkins.

"What's that? Oh! I haven't?"

"No! What do *you* think about the danger of radiation?"

"I thought I already answered that," said Mr. Hawkins, mopping his brow with a huge, colored handkerchief.

"Okay! Let me ask you another question. Do you think the Air Force has done all that it could to try and locate the bomb? In other words, are you satisfied, Mr. Congressman, with the search the Air Force has conducted up to this point?"

"Would you repeat that, please?"

"Do you think the Air Force is doing a good job, Congressman Hawkins?"

"Oh, yes! Yes! The Air Force always does a good job. Fine organization. Fine organization."

"But, do you think they've done a good job in trying to find this bomb?"

"Well...they haven't found it yet, have they?"

It was Mr. Jenkins's turn to mop his forehead. "Let me ask you another question, sir. Do you think there is any possibility these kids may have found the bomb...and the Air Force just won't listen to them?"

"Anything is possible in a free society," said the congressman, shifting his feet again. "That's the democratic way! I have said, time and time again...."

"Mr. Congressman! Would you mind answering the question?" Jenkins interrupted. "Do you think these kids may actually know the location of the bomb?"

"I was just getting to that! As I was saying...." and Mr. Hawkins pulled Henry closer to him and patted him on the head again, "...we must look to the youth of this country for answers to the problems of the future, and I...."

"Thank you, very much, Mr. Congressman," said Jenkins, snatching the microphone out of his hand. "Thank you...This is Richard Jenkins of WSEE-TV at the Town Hall in Mammoth Falls, where we have just been talking to Congressman Seth Hawkins...."

By this time, Henry was so fed up you could see his ears beginning to stick out from under the thick mop of hair that usually covers them. He got himself out from under Congressman Hawkins' sweaty arm and snatched the map away from Mr. Jenkins. Then he stomped down the Town Hall steps and took off across the lawn. Several of the reporters took off after him. You seldom see Henry get mad. But when he does his scalp sort of jerks back and forth and his eyebrows jump up and down because he keeps wrinkling his forehead into a deep frown. And his eyes look as though they could burn a hole right through a concrete wall. And Henry Mulligan was certainly mad this time. He kept right on going across the lawn, across the street, and across the town square, until the reporters caught up with him at the base of Hannah Kimball's statue.

Naturally, we all took off after Henry too; but we had to fight our way through what looked like an ocean of umbrellas with women hanging from them, and it wasn't easy. Harmon, who doesn't care what people think of him, solved the problem by hollering, "Look out! I gotta vomit!", and he got a quicker reaction than a buffalo hunter splitting a herd. A path six feet wide opened up in front of him, and Jeff and Mortimer and I managed to scramble through right behind him before the gap closed again. Homer is a little clumsy, though, and he got clobbered with umbrellas, because he stepped on a woman's foot.

When we caught up with them, the reporters had Henry backed up against the base of the statue and were peppering him with questions. Mr. Jenkins came puffing up behind us and pushed his way in among them. He had a hard time getting through the umbrellas, too, because blood was trickling down his cheek from a cut over his right eye, and the shirt had been torn half off his back.

"Henry," he panted, "do you really know where that bomb is?"

"I don't know, for sure," said Henry, brushing aside another reporter's question. "A real scientist is never sure until he has all the facts in hand. But we do know there is a large metal object in the lake right where Jeff and Charlie heard something splash in the water while that scramble was going on. That much we can prove."

"How do you know that, kiddo?" asked a stocky reporter with his coat slung over his arm.

"Because of the anomaly."

"What's this *anomaly* you keep talking about, sonny?"

Henry picked his nose. "An anomaly is anything that's abnormal. In this case it's a disturbance in the regular pattern of the flux lines of the earth's magnetic field."

"That's just what I thought it was," quipped another reporter, and everyone gave him the horselaugh.

"Are you a scientist?" asked the stocky reporter.

Henry looked a little sheepish. "Well, I guess I'm not, yet...but I hope to be when I grow up."

"Well, how you gonna prove where this thing is?"

A gleam came into Henry's eyes and he looked at his watch. Then he looked up into the top branches of the elm trees surrounding Hannah Kimball's statue and stroked his chin.

"Well? How you gonna prove it?" another reporter asked.

"Shut up!" said Harmon Muldoon. "You don't talk while a scientist's thinking! 'Specially Henry!"

"Oh! I beg your august pardon," said the reporter, with an elaborate, sweeping bow that took in both Harmon and Henry. "After this, I'll ask your permission before I ask a question."

"Don't mention it!" said Harmon, blowing on his fingernails.

"But I still want to know how you're gonna prove it!" the reporter repeated, looking straight at Henry.

By this time Henry had brought his eyes down from the trees, and the gleam was in them again. He turned to Mr. Jenkins. "Can you be at the dock in front of the Crocker's cabin at Strawberry Lake at eight o'clock tomorrow morning?"

"I'll be there if you've got something to show me," said Mr. Jenkins, "but the police will probably run us off."

"I don't think they'll run us off if there are enough reporters there," said Henry, looking around.

"I'll be there," said the man with the coat slung over his arm. "I've never seen a real scientist at work," he added, with a wink to one of his colleagues. "Especially a *mad* scientist!"

"Count me in, too," said several others.

"Henry, if you can show us anything at all, you'll have every reporter in town there," said Mr. Jenkins. "All we're getting from the Air Force is talk, and my news director is climbing all over me!"

"What about pictures, Jenkins," said the little cameraman, poking him in the ribs.

"Yeah! What about pictures Henry? We're dead if we don't have something to photograph."

"If everything goes well, you'll get some pictures," said Henry.

"What do you mean, if everything goes well?"

"You'll find out tomorrow morning," said Henry. "C'mon Jeff, we've got a lot of work to do." And Henry took off across the square to where our bicycles were parked, with the rest of us scrambling after him.

The Trout the Size of a Whale

I will never forget that night, nor the morning that followed. When Henry Mulligan gets an idea stuck in his head, he can be a real bear. He starts giving orders right and left and you can hardly talk to him. But, as we always find out in the end, he usually knows what he's doing.

As we pedaled away from the town square, Henry was jabbering a blue streak. Most of it was directed at Jeff, but you could tell Henry expected all of us to listen to what he was saying, because he kept turning his head to see if we were keeping up.

"I didn't like that fathead calling you a *mad* scientist!" I said, when he had stopped talking long enough to catch his breath.

"I don't mind," said Henry. "Maybe it's better if they think we're a little bit kooky. Anyway, he gave me a good idea."

"Whaddaya mean? I didn't hear him say anything brilliant."

"He didn't. But when he asked me how we could prove where the bomb is, it started me thinking, and all of a sudden it just sort of came to me. If they think we're a little kooky now, wait'll they see what happens tomorrow morning."

"What's gonna happen?" asked Harmon Muldoon.

"Wait 'til we get to Jeff's barn," said Henry. "We can't afford to let anybody know what we're doing, so we have to be careful about who's listening in."

"You mean this is a Top Secret operation?"

"Yeah, this is Top Secret, all right," said Henry, "if that makes you any happier."

"Oh, boy!" said Harmon. "Wait'll I tell that dopey cousin of mine."

"Harmon, you've got a head like a Hubbard squash!" said Jeff. "Hard on the outside, and soft on the inside! Henry just told you we can't let anybody know what we're doing. And that includes your cousin!"

"Horsefeathers!" said Harmon. "What good is a secret if you can't tell anybody about it?"

Nobody answered him, and we just kept on pedaling until we got to Jeff's place and locked ourselves in the tack room.

"What about this cousin of yours, Harmon?" Henry asked as he settled himself on the old piano stool and hooked his toes in behind the legs. "Could we trust him? We're gonna need some extra help tonight."

"You can trust him as long as you feed him," said Harmon. "Like I told Jeff, he eats a lot."

"But if we let him in on what we're doing, will he go blabbing it all over town?"

"How's he gonna know what we're doing, if I don't know myself?"

"Okay! Okay!" said Henry. "I'll tell you what we're gonna do as soon as I've figured it out. Meanwhile, you go get your cousin. We're gonna need all the help we can get."

"And don't forget to give the password when you come back," said Mortimer. " 'Cause you won't get in without it."

"Okay! What is it?"

"We haven't figured that out yet, either. But we'll know when you get back!"

Harmon pulled a moldy old saddle off a peg on the wall and threw it right at Mortimer, who caught it like a basketball and sent it flying right back so fast that Harmon barely got out the door before it thudded against the door panel. From outside came one of Harmon's loudest raspberries, as he mounted his bicycle and headed for town.

"That's enough horseplay!" said Jeff. "We've got a lot of work to do. How about giving out with the plan, Henry?"

Henry was staring up into the darkness of the rafters again, but he came to right away and took his glasses off to wipe them. "Well, as I see the situation," he said quietly, "we've got to do something dramatic to convince people we know what we're talking about. Otherwise, we're not going to get anywhere. But the *first* thing we have to do is prove to ourselves that we know what we're talking about...and that means *we have got to find the bomb!*"

"How we gonna do that?" Homer sneered. "With the lake practically crawlin' with police launches, and maybe full of radiation, and the water maybe more than a hundred feet deep out there...a fat chance we got!"

Henry had that faint smile around his lips that he always has when somebody is letting the stupidity run out of his mouth like Homer was, and he took a little time to blow very carefully on one lens of his glasses. "I believe a few corrections are in order," he said, as he fitted the glasses back over his eyes. "Item: We've already proved the police have very little chance of catching us if we work at night. Item: Like I told Mr. Jenkins, if there was any dangerous radiation on the lake, the police wouldn't be out there. And, anyway, it would have shown up on our Geiger counter, which it obviously didn't. Item: Jeff told me that their anchor hit bottom at thirty feet when he and Harmon and Charlie rowed back out there to dive, and got chased off the lake by Chief Putney."

Homer looked a little abashed. But then, he couldn't be expected to know everything that Henry does. "Oh, *excuse me!*" he said, bowing from the waist with the palms of his hands pressed flat against each other in front of his nose. "But if everything is so hunky-dory, would your Majestic Presence please explain what we're supposed to do?" Homer reads a lot and can get very flowery.

"Well, it isn't going to be easy," said Henry. "That's why we need more help, and why we've got to be well organized. I think we ought to decide right now who's going to be giving the orders, and who's responsible for what, so there aren't any slip-ups."

"That's a good idea," said Mortimer. "Why don't we hold an election while Harmon's gone so we can tell him who's president as soon as he gets back?"

"Why don't we form a club? Then we can have a charter, and a constitution, and by-laws, and all that stuff!" said Homer. "And we can vote on everything, and...."

"What about a Bill of Rights?" I shouted, trying to drown out Homer. "If you don't have a Bill of Rights, you ain't got nothin'."

"Phooey!" said Mortimer. "That causes too many arguments. What we do need is a secret grip. I know a dandy!"

"How about a few campaign speeches?" Homer shouted, jumping up on the saddle rail at the end of the room. "When in the course of human events our fathers brought forth on this continent a more perfect Union, to establish justice, insure domestic tranquility, and create all men equal...."

"Hey! You're all mixed up, Homer!" Jeff hollered above the general din. And he pounded for order on the packing crate in front of him with a rusty stirrup.

All of a sudden it was quiet in the tack room, and Mortimer said in a squeaky voice, "I vote for Jeff for President!"

"I second the motion!" I said. "And I nominate Henry Mulligan as Vice President and Chief Scientist."

"That's O.K. by me," said Homer, as he jumped down from the saddle rail.

"I move we make it magnanimous," said Mortimer.

"I think you mean *u*nanimous," Henry said, with that faint smile on his face again.

"No I don't," said Mortimer. "But you're the Vice President. Make it '*u*nanimous'. It'll sound better in the minutes of the first meeting."

And that's how the Mad Scientists' Club got

organized...if you want to call it that. By the time Harmon Muldoon showed up with his cousin Freddy, we had everything settled and Homer was taking notes on the side of a cardboard soup carton. We still have that soup carton in our museum, along with the big dinosaur egg we found, some leftover skin from The Strange Sea Monster, the control system for The Flying Sorcerer, and a lot of other junk. The Unidentified Flying Man of Mammoth Falls, of course, still stands in the window of Mike Corcoran's Idle Hour Pool Hall on Blake Street, because we let him borrow it permanently.

When Harmon came busting through the door of the tack room he had two other kids with him, instead of just one. One of them was a skinny little kid with a thatch of stiff, blond hair, and some freckles on his nose. We all knew he couldn't be Harmon's cousin.

"The fat one's my cousin Freddy," said Harmon, by way of introduction. "This here kid is Dinky Poore. He don't look like much, but he can crawl through a twelve-inch pipe, or shinny all the way up a flag pole before you can count ten. Freddy wouldn't come unless Dinky came too, so here he is." And Harmon sat down on a box and fanned himself.

"How did you manage to bust that door open?" said Mortimer.

"I didn't know the password, so I used my head!" Harmon shot back.

Freddy Muldoon flopped down on an old peach basket and began fanning himself, too, but Dinky Poore just stood stiff against the wall near the door and rubbed his nose and kept looking out the windows and up at the ceiling and any place except at the rest of us.

I wouldn't say he was self-conscious, or anything, but he just looked as if he wished he could hide behind something, or just drop through the floor.

"How about telling us what we're supposed to do now, Henry?" said Harmon, after he had gotten his breath. "Freddy can't talk much, 'cause he's got a sore throat, and Dinky, here, is too scared to talk, so I don't think you got much to worry about."

"Wait a minute!" said Jeff, pounding on the crate again with the rusty stirrup. "I forgot to tell you, Harmon, but we had a little meeting while you were gone and I was elected President. So *I'll* decide what the order of business is, and who's going to talk."

"How many votes did you get?" said Harmon.

"He got five," Mortimer chimed in. "We knew you'd vote for yourself, so we gave you one vote, and it came out five-to-one in favor of Jeff."

"That figures!" said Harmon "At least I know you guys can add."

"Okay!" said Jeff. "Now, how about telling us what we're supposed to do now, Henry?"

"Well, as I was saying, the first thing we've got to do is prove to ourselves that we know where the bomb is," said Henry. "So that means we've got to go out there and dive in that area where we got the strong reading on the magnetometer. We know that we can only do it at night, and I propose that we do it right away."

"You mean tonight?" asked Harmon.

"Tonight!" said Henry. "We've got all afternoon to get ready, but we've got a lot of work to do and a lot of equipment to get together. The way I see it, we're going to need two boats, and we'll have to take the magnetometer along to make sure we have the right location...and we're going to need at least three guys with scuba gear to do the diving...and I've got to run over to Clinton and borrow an underwater camera from a friend of mine...and we've got to set up the same beacon transmitters on the shore...and we've got to get some nylon line and a big balloon with a gas pellet in it, and a couple of small detonators, and... well, I can't read off everything now, but I made up a list while we were waiting for Harmon to get back, and what we have to do now is decide who is going to do what."

Dinky Poore had stopped looking out the windows. He was staring at Henry with his eyes bugged out of his head like a frog's and he even forgot to rub his nose. Homer was taking notes so fast he already had two sides of the soup carton covered, and he was waving at Henry to knock it off for a minute.

"Okay, okay!" said Jeff. "We better send Homer out right away to set up the beacon on the north shore of the lake, so he can get back here in time to help with some of the other stuff. The one in our cottage is still there, so all we have to do is sneak somebody in there after dark to turn it on. Harmon better do that."

"We still got your boat stashed in that cove on the peninsula," said Mortimer. "Where we gonna get another one?"

"We'll just borrow one," said Jeff. "There's plenty of good boats tied up at the docks near our cottage, and nobody can use 'em right now, so they won't even know we borrowed one. The only thing is, we won't have a motor for it."

Dinky Poore raised his right hand timidly. "My old man's got a motor," he said in a squeaky voice.

Everybody turned to look at him, and he turned red
right up to the roots of his hair.

"What kind is it?" asked Jeff.

"I don't know, but it don't make much noise at all
'cause he got it for bass fishin' in the bulrushes. I can
lift it real easy."

"Then it's small enough!" said Henry. "Will your dad
let us borrow it?"

"Sure!" said Dinky, proudly. Then he frowned. "But
we better go get it before he gets home."

"Oh, by all means," said Mortimer. "We wouldn't
wanna disturb him."

"All right!" said Jeff. "You go with Dinky and pick up
his motor, Mortimer, and bring it here. Harmon and I
will take it down to the lake with us tonight, and when
it's dark enough, we'll snitch a boat and take off
straight across the lake to the peninsula. What else,
Henry?"

"The rest of us will have to get the scuba gear and all
the radio equipment out there," said Henry, "and I
don't know whether we can get all that stuff up over
the ridge and down to the cove where we left your boat.
That's a pretty stiff climb. I think we need another
plan, Jeff."

"Okay, what do you suggest?"

"How about meeting us at that little beach near
Turkey Hill Road, where we started from before?" said
Homer. "Then you and Harmon could take us all over
to the peninsula in that boat you filch."

"Forget it, forget it, little pea-brain!" said Harmon.
"We almost got caught there the last time, before we
even got started. It's too exposed. Besides, that…as
light as your head is, I don't think one boat will carry

eight of us and all that junk Henry's been drivelin' about."

"I don't know how he figured it out, but Harmon's right," said Jeff. "We gotta think of something else."

"I think I know what we can do," Henry said, gazing up at the rafters again and stroking his chin. "We'll follow Turkey Hill Road out to where it curves around the north end of the lake. Right where the old railroad track from the zinc mine crosses the road, there's a little dirt trail that leads down into the swampy end of the lake. From there, it's not very far by water over to the peninsula. It's too shallow for the patrol boat to get back in there, so I think it's an ideal place to operate from."

"Sounds great!" said Jeff.

"Now, here's what I think we can do," Henry continued. And he leaned forward until the front legs of his stool hit the floor, and he started drawing a diagram in the dust with his finger. "We can go out Turkey Hill Road to here, and Mortimer and Dinky can climb over the ridge from there and get your boat out of the bushes by that cove. We'll take their bikes with us and go on up to the north end of the lake. Right about here—and I'll show you the place on the map—you can meet us with both boats. Homer can meet us there, too, after he's set up the beacon transmitter on the north shore. That means he won't have to start out so soon, and he can help us get some of this stuff together."

"That's usin' the old noodle, Henry!" said Mortimer. "I'm in favor of Homer doing more work."

"You must be better'n Julius Caesar, the way you dope this stuff out," said Freddy Muldoon, gazing at Henry with admiration. "What do they call you? Henry the First?"

Right then I knew that Freddy would qualify as a member of the club.

That night, just at dusk, all of us except Jeff and Harmon were pedaling along Turkey Hill Road with our bikes loaded down with diving and radio gear, and Homer was scrambling through the woods somewhere on the north shore of the lake to set up the beacon transmitter by the benchmark. We hadn't gone more than two miles before I noticed that Dinky Poore kept lagging behind, and I had to keep circling back to make him pedal faster and keep up with the rest of us. Finally, I had to take most of Dinky's load and strap part of it on my handlebars so he could keep up. It was easy to see what Dinky's trouble was. His bike didn't match his trousers. He wouldn't ride a twenty-six inch bike, because everybody would think he was a little kid. So he got his old man to buy him a twenty-eight inch bike, and when he sat on the seat, his feet wouldn't reach the pedals. Wherever he went, Dinky had to ride standing up, and that can get old pretty fast.

Fortunately, it wasn't too far to the place where Mortimer and Dinky had to climb over the ridge to the cove where we'd left Jeff's boat. Dinky made it there in good shape, and he and Mortimer plunged into the bushes at the side of the road and started their climb. The rest of us went on, taking turns at wheeling their bikes along with us.

By the time we reached the abandoned railroad track to the zinc mine, it was completely dark. Henry pulled off to the left of the road, got off his bike, and started down a narrow path that paralleled the track.

"Hurry up!" he said in a hoarse whisper. "Everybody off the road before a car comes along and somebody sees us!"

No sooner had he said it than we heard the screech-
ing tires of a car taking a curve at high speed, and
Turkey Hill Road was suddenly illuminated by its head-
lights. I dove into the bushes, pulling my bike after me.
But Freddy Muldoon isn't used to moving fast, and he
was standing on the apron of the road with his fat face
hanging out when the car rounded the curve and
caught him in the beam of its lights. It was an Air
Force sedan, and the driver slammed on his brakes
when he saw Freddy and came to a screaming halt
about two hundred feet down the road.

"Stay where you are, Freddy!" I hissed, in a stage
whisper. "Whatever you do, don't run! Tell 'em you're
just on your way home from Clinton."

The car started backing up, and somebody on the
passenger side stuck a high-powered flashlight out the
window and trained it on Freddy. What he saw was
Freddy leaning on his bike and munching a banana
he'd pulled out of his shirt. There were two Air Police
in the car, and when they pulled up beside Freddy the
one with the flashlight said, "What are you doing way
out here, Sonny?"

"I'm eating a banana," said Freddy.

"I can see that, smart aleck!" said the Air Policeman.
"What I want to know is what you're doing out here all
by yourself?"

"I got hungry," said Freddy, "so I stopped to eat a
banana before I got home."

"Where do you live?" the other Air Policeman asked
him.

"In Mammoth Falls, mostly," said Freddy. "But
sometimes I go over to Clinton and bother some

people I know."

Meanwhile, the airman with the flashlight was sweeping the bushes with it, making sure there was no one else with Freddy. I held my breath and tried not to move a muscle, hoping that the leaves I'd pulled over my bicycle covered all the bright metal on it that might send back a reflection.

"You *are* a smart aleck!" said the driver. "What's all that stuff you have on your bike?"

"You got a warrant?" Freddy asked, cramming his mouth full of banana.

The man with the flashlight burst out laughing and flicked his light off. "He's got you there, Hardy!" he said. "Come on. Let's get going."

"Okay, okay!" said the driver. "But, look, kiddo. Get yourself on home right away. We gotta patrol this road to keep people from getting through to Strawberry Lake. That's the only reason we're asking you questions. You heard about the bomb, I suppose?"

"I heard about it," said Freddy.

"Okay! Look! Why don't you stick your bike in the trunk and hop in. We'll get you home a lot sooner. You have a long way to pedal, yet."

"No thanks," said Freddy. "My mother told me never to take rides with strangers."

"Oh, horsefeathers!" said the driver. And, he put his car in gear and took off down the road toward town.

"They were pretty nice guys, but kinda stupid," said Freddy, as he and I made our way down the path to join Henry. Little did we know how nice they were, at the time. Because they came back up the road a little later to see if Freddy was getting home all right, and they couldn't find him.

"That was close!" said Henry, when we rejoined him. "But you did just the right thing, Freddy. You did just fine."

"I don't never have no trouble with cops," Freddy observed. "I like talkin' to 'em."

A few yards down the path we came to an old wagon trail that jutted off to the left of the track, and we could mount our bikes again. It was pretty overgrown, and the tree branches hung pretty low in a lot of places; but it had a white sand surface, so we could see our way without too much difficulty.

"Keep close together!" Henry cautioned in a low voice, as we picked our way carefully down the trail. "There are some forks along here, I remember, that lead into peat bogs. If we lose sight of each other, somebody might get lost. And no flashlights! You never can tell when a light might be seen from the lake."

We rode slowly along, with the only sounds coming from the soft squish of our tires in the sand, and an occasional burp from Freddy.

"I wish you'd stop burping," I hissed at him. "Every time you do, I can smell bananas. Cops have noses, too, you know. You wanna give away our position?"

"That's what I like about bananas," he grunted. "They still taste good, long after you ate 'em."

"By the way, what did you do with the skin from that last one?"

"I threw it in the back seat of the Air Police car while they were laughin' at me."

"Shut up, you guys!" Henry said, tersely. "We're getting near the swamps now. Let's keep a sharp eye out."

Homer was already there when we reached the place Henry had chosen as a rendezvous point. It was a dry hummock that jutted out into a large, fairly clear section of the main swamp. And, though it was completely masked from the lake itself by tall swamp growth and occasional islands, there was a narrow channel you could follow, if you knew the way, that brought you out into open water in about a quarter of a mile. The hummock had a few large trees on it, and a lot of scrub and bush growth around its edges that completely hid a small clearing out near the end facing the lake. From there, it was only a few hundred feet through the brush back to where the old wagon trail skirted the swamp. We could easily hack a narrow path through the brush if we had to, and the brush was thick enough so the path couldn't be seen from any direction. It was an ideal place to operate from, for the purposes we had in mind, and we owed its discovery to Henry. He likes to go rambling through the woods collecting rare plants and butterflies, and he really knows the shores of Strawberry Lake like nobody else in Mammoth Falls.

Homer was sitting at one edge of the clearing with his back up against a big rock and rubbernecking nervously from side to side. Freddy just had to burp, of course, when we were about twenty feet from him, and Homer sprang to his feet as though a red ant had bitten him.

"Who's that?" he wailed, in a high, squeaky voice.

"Tippecanoe!" said Henry.

"Skinamaroo!" Homer sighed in relief, and we stepped out into the clearing.

"Jeepers, but it's spooky here!" Homer said, lamely. "I been waitin' more'n half an hour. Where you guys been?"

"We were detained by military authorities," said

Freddy Muldoon. "What excuse do you have?"

"I don't need no excuse. I been here all the time."

"You couldn't have been here more than ten minutes, Homer," Henry said, quietly. "It's just nine o'clock, and I think we've made good time. Now, if the two boats show up soon, we'll be right on schedule."

"How they gonna find their way through this swamp from out there on the lake?" Freddy asked.

"That's not too difficult," said Henry as he rummaged through the big duffel bag he had lugged through the brush with him. "You see this?"

"Looks like some kind of a light," said Freddy. "What is it?"

"It's some kind of a light, all right," said Henry. "Specifically, it's an infrared light. You can't see it with the naked eye, but if you look at it through an infrared filter that absorbs all the other kinds of light, then you can see it."

"Holy mackerel!" said Freddy. "You're a genius, Henry!"

"No, I'm not. But I want to be," said Henry. "Now start wiring these batteries in series so we have enough voltage to make this thing glow. Homer! Get up in that big oak tree over there and find an open place where you can aim this light out toward the lake."

Freddy didn't know what Henry meant by "in series" but with a little help from me he got the batteries wired properly, and connected to the light that Homer took up into the tree with him at the end of a long wire.

"Last time I saw Jeff he had naked eyes," Freddy muttered, half to himself. "How's he gonna see this stupid light?"

"Both he and Mortimer have field glasses fitted with

infrared filters," Henry explained. "They'll see it, all right."

"Holy Moses! You think of everything, Henry."

"Somebody has to," said Henry. "That's what makes the difference between a good operation and a big flop. Charlie! Turn on your radio. They may want to be contacting us pretty soon."

I switched on the handset and listened, but there was nothing but a hum and some static coming in.

"All we can do now is wait," said Henry.

We didn't have to wait long. Pretty soon I thought I sure could hear a faint hum coming from the direction of the lake, and it sounded like a small outboard motor. I tried a call on the radio.

"Mugwump! This is High Mogul! Come in, please."

"This is Mugwump!" came the reply. "Go ahead!"

It was Jeff. I turned the radio over to Henry and he asked Jeff if he knew where Mortimer and Dinky were.

"I hope that's them putting along somewhere behind us," said Jeff. "If it isn't, we're in trouble, because somebody is following us!"

"Keep cool, Mugwump," said Henry. "If that was company they'd have a light on you by now."

"Hello, you old High Mogul!" said another voice. "This is Walrus! Get ready to drag the lake. We're coming in low!"

"Watch what you're saying!" said Henry. "You don't know who's listening in."

"Excuse me!" said Mortimer. "Make that 'Lay out the mats! We're right on course.' "

"That's better," said Henry.

Between the infrared beacon, and Henry's directions on the radio, both Jeff and Mortimer managed to guide their boats through the maze of tiny islands and channels in the swamp and nosed them into a small cleft in the bank of the hummock. We loaded all the equipment aboard, and then we all sat in a tight circle in the little clearing while Henry gave us his final instructions.

"Jeff, Mortimer, and Charlie are going to do the diving," he said, "and it's up to the rest of us to see that they get back up to the surface safely. We'll use lines to keep track of where they are, and to send signals. Also, they'll tie themselves together so they can't get into trouble without the other two knowing about it. You can't be too careful diving at night. Jeff and Mortimer will go down first, and then Charlie will spell one of them for the next dive. If they find the bomb, Charlie will go down with the camera and try to get a picture. There's only one hitch."

"What's that?" said Homer.

"If that police launch shows up while the divers are down, the only thing we can do is run for it and try to get back to that same cove we ducked into last night. That means we'll have to cut the lines, and it's every man for himself. Four jerks on the line will mean there's trouble on the surface, and the divers will have to make for the peninsula on their own."

"Thanks a lot!" said Mortimer. "I don't think we discussed this when you signed me up."

"We didn't," Henry admitted. "But we didn't have time for everything. Besides...if I'd told you about it then, you might have decided not to come."

"Boy, that Henry, he thinks of everything!" Freddy Muldoon whispered to Dinky Poore, who was sitting there with his mouth open. Dinky nodded and started to answer, but just then a mosquito flew down his throat and all he could do was cough and make gurgling sounds.

"I figure it's no more than three hundred yards to the nose of the peninsula," said Jeff. "If we can't make that, we shouldn't be diving."

"I don't think you'll have any trouble if you stay underwater until the police launch passes by," said Henry. "We'll lead it around to the west side of the peninsula. Then you can surface and make for shore."

"I hope it's a fast chase," Mortimer added. "We only have thirty minutes of air in each tank."

"That's enough, if you don't breathe," said Harmon.

"That'd be a good time to take up drinking!" Homer snickered, as Henry and Jeff led the way toward the two boats.

Jeff and Mortimer and I got into one boat with Freddy Muldoon and all the diving gear. The other boat was the control boat, with Harmon in charge of handling the diving lines, Homer in charge of the directional radio receivers, and Henry in charge of everything. Dinky Poore sat in the stern, getting instructions from Henry on how to read the dial on the magnetometer.

We had wrapped strips of burlap around the oarlocks, so we crept out of the swamp very quietly on our way toward open water. We didn't intend to use the motors unless we had to run for it, and it looked as if we wouldn't have to. Not only was there no moon, but a slight ground mist had begun to develop and there were wisps of it floating just above the surface of the water. It wouldn't bother us, but if it got any worse the patrol boat would have a hard time seeing anything on the lake, and might not even be able to navigate.

"This ought to get thicker when the temperature drops a little more, and I sure hope it does," said Henry, as we nosed out onto the lake.

We didn't know it then, but the name of Henry Mulligan had provided dinner table conversation in millions of homes throughout the country that evening. The Mammoth Falls *Gazette* figured the women's protest march on the Town Hall was the big news of the day. But evening papers elsewhere in the country had carried a tongue-in-cheek news story headlined: LOCAL 'SCIENTIST' SAYS HE KNOWS WHERE BOMB IS! When people showed us copies of the story a few days later, it kinda burned us up, but by then we were too busy to worry about it. Besides, Henry had already made the reporter who wrote it look like a fool.

We made our way very slowly out to the area off the nose of the peninsula, keeping a sharp eye out for signs of the patrol boat. Henry had ordered no talking, so we could listen for sounds of a motor; and between the silence and the mist I had the eerie feeling we were crossing the River Styx into another world. And maybe we were, for all any of us knew. Here we were out on a lake we weren't supposed to be on, heading for an area none of us had ever dived in before, and at the bottom—if we were lucky—we'd find an atom bomb that could blow the whole town of Mammoth Falls to kingdom come if anything went wrong.

When we got to the point a few hundred yards off the nose of the peninsula where we had to start locating our position precisely, everybody was a little bit jumpy. Especially because Homer kept jockeying the control boat back and forth, and around in circles, while he tried to home in on the two beacon transmitters we had left on the shore. Finally, Henry had to tell him how to do it: by homing in on one signal, taking a compass reading to verify it, and then proceeding directly along that line until we intercepted the signal from the other beacon. I was in a nervous sweat and beginning to feel a clammy chill creeping over my body. And I wasn't the only one. I noticed that both Mortimer and Jeff were shivering as they strapped their tanks on their backs. But Freddy Muldoon was just sitting there with the butt ends of the oars in his lap, picking his nose.

Finally, Henry checked the reading on the magnetometer and we dropped anchor. Again they hit bottom at about thirty feet.

"You guys were right. It is shallow here," said Henry.

Jeff and Mortimer slipped over the side of our boat and let themselves noiselessly into the water. I handed them their lights and clipped the lines to them, while Harmon and Freddy lashed the two boats together. Then Jeff and Mortimer did a porpoise dive and disappeared silently in the dark waters of the lake. I could see their lights sinking deeper in the water. They were tiny pinpoints of light for awhile, surrounded by wide circles of light. Then, as they got deeper and the water became murkier, there was just a dull glow that gave us only an approximate idea of where the divers were. We waited and tried to keep quiet.

It was about ten minutes before Mortimer came up and clambered into the boat. "You go down for awhile, Charlie," he told me, "I want to talk with Henry."

"What do you see down there? Anything?" I asked him.

"It drops off sharply right over there," he said,

pointing toward the stern of the boat. "It looks like a steep cliff. We went down pretty far, but we don't know how far it is to the bottom. May be a pretty deep hole."

"I don't think it's a hole," said Henry. "I think the whole lake is deep in this area. We're probably anchored over an underwater ridge that comes off that peninsula. That's why it's shallow right here."

"Maybe so," said Mortimer. "But Jeff wants you to drop a light on a plumb line, so we can tell where we are."

"Good idea!" Henry agreed. "We should have thought of that in the first place."

I dropped over the side and followed Jeff's line down to where I found him resting on a ledge of the cliff Mortimer had told us about. In less than a minute we saw the light dropping slowly toward us, but it went out of sight somewhere above us. Jeff signaled me to shine my flashlight upward, and he went up and snared the light from the top of the cliff where it had landed and brought it down to the ledge. Then he gave two pulls on the line and Henry let the light drop farther down the face of the cliff until Jeff signaled him to stop with two jerks on the line. Then Jeff motioned to me, and we both dove downward. I could feel the water getting colder and the pressure on my ears getting stronger, and pretty soon I just had to pull up short and wait to get used to it. I was glad to see Jeff giving the "level off" signal at the same time, because I don't think I could have gone any deeper just then. I don't know how deep we were, but there wasn't any sign of the bottom when we shone our lights down. Out of the corner of my eye I could see Jeff motioning to knock it off.

We started back up the face of the cliff very slowly,

to allow plenty of time for decompression, and we stopped about halfway up to rest on another ledge. It was a pretty broad ledge, with a lot of tall weeds growing on it, and while we sat there I couldn't help thinking about what a stupid flop our whole expedition was turning out to be. The bomb was obviously in such deep water that it would take hard hat equipment to get to it—if it was there at all—and we might as well pack up all our gear and crawl home. I could already hear all those reporters laughing at us and making wisecracks about Henry's fancy map, and his magical "magnometer."

Just then something brushed past my face mask, and I looked up to see the biggest lake trout I have ever seen in my life. It had come out of the weeds like a flash and darted right between Jeff and me. I figured it must be the giant trout that fishermen around Mammoth Falls call Old Pincushion. Nobody has ever been able to catch him, and they never have known what part of the lake to find him in. He just shows up occasionally, grabs somebody's line, and runs off with it. Some people figure he must have twenty or thirty hooks in him.

I looked at Jeff, and he was looking at me and jabbing his finger back toward the weeds Old Pincushion had come from. Another giant trout came flashing out. He was the second biggest lake trout I had ever seen in my life and he slithered away into the darkness in no time. I had almost forgotten about the bomb. I figured Jeff and I had stumbled on the hiding place of Old Pincushion, and maybe a whole tribe of giant lake trout, for all I knew. We both started pawing at the weeds with our hands, and two more big trout came

flying out of there. Then Jeff started crawling through
the weeds on his knees with his light stuck out in front
of him, and I wriggled along behind him. When we got
to the face of the cliff it wasn't there. Suddenly there
were no more weeds—but there wasn't any cliff,
either, and we sort of tumbled into a big, black hole.

Both of us back-pedaled and stuck our flippers out
in front of us to slow us down. You don't nose your way
into strange holes underwater unless you know where
you're going, because you might not be able to get out.
The first thing to do was back up, and try to get our
bearings. We kicked our way back to where the thick
growth of weeds had ended and flashed our lights
around to try and locate the face of the cliff. It didn't
take long to discover that we had stumbled onto what
appeared to be the mouth of a cave, hidden from view
by the tall growth of weeds on the ledge. Jeff signaled
to me that he would stay at the mouth while I swam
inside at the end of a line to take a look.

We had about forty feet of line tying us together, but
I didn't need it all, because I came up against the back
wall of the cave after I'd gone no more than twenty
feet. Two more trout skipped out from behind a rock
right beside me and dove toward the floor of the cave.
I swung the beam of my torch down and what I saw
made my heart flip over twice. It looked like a trout the
size of a whale! It was just lying there, stone still on the
sandy bottom, and my legs suddenly felt as if they had
been frozen stiff. All I knew was I didn't want to be in
the same cave with a trout that big, and I shot out of
there like something out of a harpoon gun. I crashed
right into Jeff at the mouth of the cave before I
regained my senses, and I felt like a fool. I realized,

then, that I had spooked myself. I had been thinking so much about Old Pincushion, and a secret hideout for giant trout, that I had forgotten all about what we were after. What I had actually seen on the sandy floor of that cave was probably *the atom bomb!*

I motioned frantically to Jeff, and he followed me back into the cave. I backed off before I reached the rear wall, signaled Jeff to stay high in the water, and beamed my light at the floor. Jeff pointed his light after mine, and we both looked at a bright metal object, about ten feet long, that looked something like a very fat cigar. There was no doubt about it. It was the lost atom bomb, that had somehow hit the water at just the right angle to carry it into this cave before it could get to the bottom of the lake.

Looking at it there, as we tread water above it, it seemed perfectly harmless. But then I began to realize what it actually was, and I had the same feeling that hit me when I thought it was a giant fish. I just wanted to get out of there before the thing went off. I looked at Jeff, and I could tell he had the same feeling. He was already backing water toward the mouth of the cave. If there was anything that Henry had drilled into us over and over again, it was the fact that we shouldn't go anywhere near the bomb if we found it. Right then, both of us agreed with him.

Once out of the cave, Jeff signaled me to stay in place while he slithered through the weeds to get the light. He brought it back and we tied the drop line to a jagged rock at the mouth of the cave, and then we both went up the line to the surface.

You can imagine the frustration among the rest of the gang when we told them we'd found the bomb, and they wanted to jump around and scream and holler and shout "Whoopee!" but they couldn't because Jeff and Henry kept telling everybody to shut up and stop rocking the boats. We spent five minutes talking over what we had to do next, while everybody kept glancing over their shoulders to see if there was any sign of the patrol boat. I checked out the underwater camera and made sure there was still enough air in my tank, and Mortimer went over his instructions with Henry three times. Jeff threw a blanket around his shoulders and wedged himself into the prow of the divers' boat to relax.

When Mortimer and I went over the side we knew exactly what we had to do, and we knew we had to do it in a hurry. Though the mist was getting thicker, it wasn't anywhere near thick enough to keep the patrol boat from coming out; and before we dove under, Freddy Muldoon claimed he could see its searchlight combing the shore of the lake where the summer cabins are. Mortimer and I dove down, tied together on the forty-foot line. With the drop line to follow, and the light shining at the mouth of the cave, it was a cinch to get where we were going. Mortimer went in the cave with me while I took four pictures of the bomb from different angles, 'cause I had told him I didn't want to go in there alone.

Then we swam out, and I sent the camera up on a line while we set about the job of anchoring the infernal apparatus Henry had doped out to amaze the reporters. An anchor from one of the boats was lowered down to us, and we wedged it in among some rocks at the mouth of the cave and piled more rocks on top of it to make sure it wouldn't pull loose. Then we grabbed the droplight and cleared out of there.

When we got back up, Henry and Harmon had inflated an old tire tube and lashed the top of a peach basket to it. Henry was carefully tacking down some wires on the peach basket lid when we surfaced.

"Make sure this thing doesn't get wet," he cautioned as he and Harmon lowered the thing over the side.

Mortimer and I towed the contraption out to a point directly over the mouth of the cave and hooked it to the anchor line. Then we cut the line loose from the boat and got back aboard.

"What was all that junk you had on that inner tube?" I asked Henry, when I got my face mask off.

"You'll find out in the morning," Henry answered. "Right now we've got to get out of here!"

Jeff and Harmon took the oars and we started making our way slowly along the west side of the peninsula, keeping close to shore so we could duck into a cove in a hurry if we heard the patrol boat. But there wasn't too much to worry about, because the mist had begun to settle in a lot thicker now, and there was very little chance that the patrol boat could get up much speed or venture out into the remote parts of the lake. We were just about at the place where we had stashed Jeff's boat the night before, when Henry clapped his hand to his forehead and said, "Hold it! Hold it! Hold it!"

"What's up?" said Jeff, as he pulled our boat alongside. "I think we ought to keep moving, Henry. We've been lucky so far. Let's not push it."

"I forgot the receiver!" said Henry. "I forgot to turn on the receiver!"

"You did?"

"We've got to go back! That's all there is to it. We just

gotta go back!"

"See what I told ya," said Freddy Muldoon to Dinky Poore. "That Henry, he thinks of everything!"

"Okay! Okay!" said Jeff. "If you didn't turn on the receiver we wasted the whole night. We gotta go do it. But let's make it snappy!"

Then Jeff took charge, like he mostly does in a crisis. He told Henry to get into our boat, and Freddy and Mortimer got into the other one. Then he told Harmon to pull into the cove where we had hidden the boat before, and wait there until we got back. He and I each took an oar and we started pulling double-time for the nose of the peninsula.

"If we get out there and find out you *didn't* forget to turn that thing on, it's gonna be real funny!" said Jeff.

"I'll be embarrassed," Henry admitted.

"You'll be *very* embarrassed with one of these oars wrapped around your neck. Don't pull so hard, Charlie! I'm a little pooped!"

I backed off a bit, because I knew Jeff was tired, but we still made good time out to where we had left Henry's diabolical contraption floating on the tire tube. We pulled up beside it and Henry jerked a little pen flashlight out of his pocket and checked over one of the black boxes mounted on the peach basket lid.

"What about it?" asked Jeff.

"It's okay, now," said Henry.

"Now? Was it okay before?"

"No comment!" said Henry, and he sat in the stern with his arms folded while we pulled our way back to where we had left Harmon and the others.

"I figure that cost us fifteen minutes," said Jeff, as we pulled into the cove where the other boat was waiting.

"At your age, you won't miss it!" said Henry grumpily. Henry doesn't usually talk like that, but I could see he was mad at himself for the booboo he'd made, and he wasn't in much of a mood to talk to anyone. As it turned out, that extra fifteen minutes probably saved us from some real embarrassment.

When we got back to the swamp and unloaded everything, Jeff and Harmon took off across the lake again to return the boat they'd borrowed. Since the mist had really socked in by then, they figured they wouldn't have any trouble getting by the patrols on shore. We decided to leave the beacon transmitter on the north shore where it was, and pick it up the next day. So Homer came along with the rest of us on the trail to Turkey Hill Road, and that made one more to help carry all the junk we had.

We hadn't quite reached the railroad track, yet, when we heard what sounded like a police radio turned up to full volume. Every once in awhile we could hear the crackle and squawk of somebody coming on the air, followed by a lot of talk that we couldn't make out. Henry held his hand up for us to stop, and we stood there in the trail straddling our bikes. All except Dinky, of course. He sat there, teetering back and forth, with one hand holding on to the limb of a tree, wishing we'd get moving again. We must have stood there more than two minutes, listening to each other breathing and not daring to move a muscle. Homer Snodgrass has adenoid trouble, and he was wheezing so loud he sounded like a creaky old pump that needs oil.

"Can't you make that sound more like a bird call?" Mortimer finally said to him. "You're gonna give us away."

"I could. But you might get all excited and lay an egg!" Homer said through his teeth.

Freddy Muldoon cut loose with a real rumbling laugh, and a high-pitched giggle from Dinky Poore made all of us jump. But, at the same time, we could hear the police radio squawking again, and I guess that saved us for the time being.

"Everybody off the trail!" Henry ordered. "Get the bikes into the bushes! But be quiet!"

We felt our way carefully through the brush to the left of the trail and found a little sandy knoll covered with juniper and bayberry bushes where we could lay the bikes down and at least sit on our haunches without being seen.

"I guess we'd better reconnoiter what's going on up by the road," said Henry, when we all got settled.

"What's that mean?" asked Dinky.

"It means we're gonna sneak up and spy on 'em," said Mortimer. "But no gigglers allowed!"

"You mean real spyin'? Like in the movies and on TV?"

"No, I mean *real* spying," said Mortimer. "We're gonna watch what they're doing, and listen to what they're saying."

"Oh!" said Dinky.

"You might be just the one to do it," said Henry. "Can you sneak through bushes without making any noise, and shinny up trees?"

"I can do all that stuff," Dinky said, rubbing his nose.

Henry sent me with Dinky and we circled through the woods to a point high on a steep bank south of the railroad and overlooking the highway. There were no bushes near the edge of the bank, but there were two large boulders poised on the edge, so close together there was only a narrow crevice between them. And this was where Dinky came in handy. He wriggled through the grass in the shadow of the two rocks and squeezed in between them until he could see down onto the road with one eye. He came scrambling back right away with the news that he could see an Air Force sedan and a police squad car parked on the side of the road where Freddy had talked with the two Air Policemen.

"Which way are they facing?" I asked him.

"They're on this side, facing toward town."

"How many policemen are there?"

"I saw two Air Police, and two of the cops from Mammoth Falls. There might be more, though. I couldn't see everything."

"Go back again, and take a careful look," I told him. "We gotta know how many there are, and what they're doing here."

Dinky snaked back through the grass and wedged himself in between the rocks again, and just then the radio in one of the cars started squawking again. The transmission was too garbled for me to make out the words, but I could hear the officer on this end answer.

"Negative, sir!" he said. "We've searched the woods about a hundred yards deep on both sides of the road and there's just no sign of the kid. The State Police car has already left the scene, sir." Then there was a lot more noise from the radio, and pretty soon I could hear the voice of the officer again.

"Positive, sir! We're positive! Both Sergeant Hardy and I spoke to the kid, and we're sure it was right here.

We came back up the road about ten minutes later, and there wasn't any sign of him. We know he couldn't have pedaled all the way to Mammoth Falls in that time. He musta pulled off the road somewhere, but we don't know where."

Squawk! Squawk! Squawk! Then: "That's a good question, sir! We don't find any tire tracks north of the railroad, but from here into town the west shoulder is full of them. Looks like there was a lot more than one bike, but we can't tell what direction they were going." Squawk! Squawk! "I don't know, sir! Maybe the kid was lying about coming from Clinton."

Squawk! Squawk! Squawk! Squawk! Squawk! "Yes, sir!" Squawk! Squawk! Squawk! "Yes, sir!" Squawk! Squawk! Squawk! Squawk! "Yes, sir! I can appreciate that, sir. But we *didn't* imagine that banana peel we found in the back seat! Yes, sir! Very well, sir!"

That was enough for me to dope out the situation. This was the same Air Police car that had caught Freddy with his bare face hanging out just before we cut into the woods toward the wagon trail. They must have come back up the road a few minutes later and wondered why they didn't pass a fat boy pedaling a bicycle toward Mammoth Falls. Obviously they had come back again with the Mammoth Falls police to look for him.

Then I heard the voice of the Air Policeman again.

"Hey, Hardy! The captain says we're to stay here. He's sending ten men out in a van, and there's another squad car coming from Mammoth Falls. We're to search the road from here into town."

I gave a soft bobwhite call and Dinky came crawling back from the rocks.

"I guess you heard that," he said.

"I sure did! Let's get out of here."

We beat it back to the knoll by the wagon trail and reported what we'd heard. Henry rubbed his chin thoughtfully and ran some sand through his fingers.

"Any other good news, you guys?" Mortimer whispered.

"How we gonna get home?" Freddy Muldoon moaned. "Have we gotta go all the way back to that lousy swamp, Henry?"

"That wouldn't do us any good, Freddy. But I do know a way we can get out of here...with a little luck." And Henry started to draw a diagram in the sand. "The trouble is, we'll have to travel light. That means we've got to leave some of our stuff here, and hope we can pick it up later."

"Seems like we do that all the time," said Homer. "Do you plan it this way Henry?"

"We've got to lug our bicycles up over this ridge across the tracks, and we aren't going to have time to come back for anything else. If we can get across the road a little bit north of the tracks without being seen, then we can follow the railroad to White Fork Road and get home that way. Everything depends on getting across that road."

We hid everything we had in the bushes, including three of the bicycles. We'd have to double up on the ride home, because three bikes were all we figured we could wrestle up over the ridge and through the woods to the road.

We made our way across the tracks and slipped and floundered up the sandy slope on the other side, tugging the bicycles after us. Then, when we got up into the trees and bushes, we had about a hundred-foot climb to the top of the ridge. We were pretty pooped, but Henry would only let us rest for one minute, because we had to get to the road before all the reinforcements arrived. We picked our way carefully down the other side and came to the road at a point about halfway around the curve north of the tracks. We couldn't get any farther up the road, because there was a large pond to our left blocking the way.

"We'll have to cross here," Henry said, when we got to the ditch at the edge of the road. "We'll do it in a gang rush. Everybody line up facing the road."

"What's a gang rush?" Freddy asked.

"It means we go together, six abreast," Henry explained. "Then the mathematical probabilities are on our side. If we try to sneak across, one at a time, they have six chances to see us. If we all go together, shoulder-to-shoulder, then it's just like one man crossing the road and they only have *one* chance to see us."

"That Henry, he thinks of everything," said Freddy to Dinky Poore.

Henry lined us up and we waited for his signal. About three hundred feet down the road were the two patrol cars with their beacon lights flashing. Between them, they kept the road in front of us almost constantly illuminated.

"When we get to the other side, keep right on going into the woods, and follow me to the railroad tracks," Henry said, tensely. "There's no point in waiting to find out whether they saw us. Go on the count of three!"

When Henry got to three, we scrambled up the bank of the ditch and dashed across the road. Homer Snodgrass fell flat on his face, and skinned both his

knees, and Mortimer had to carry their bike by himself.
But Homer caught up with us as soon as we got into
the bushes on the other side. Down the road toward
Mammoth Falls we could hear the wail of a siren coming toward us, and we figured we had made it just in
time. Henry cautioned us to slow down, so we wouldn't
make a lot of noise, but he really didn't have to. We
found ourselves in a thicket of blackberry bushes and
we were getting scratched and snagged at every step.

"Nuts to this!" said Mortimer, and he picked up his
bike and he and Homer used it as a shield to bulldoze
a path through the brambles.

The rest of us followed until we broke out of the
thicket, and then Henry led the way down a lightly
wooded slope to where we found the old railroad track
from the zinc mine again. From there it was about two
miles to White Fork Road, and we made it in good style,
sometimes riding our bikes and sometimes pushing
them where the tracks had been overgrown with vines
and tall weeds. We rode home by way of White Fork
Road just as though we were coming back from the
carnival at the White Fork fair grounds, and nobody
bothered us.

When I got home, my mother wanted to know where
I'd been and how come my clothes were so torn and
dirty, and I told her we'd been playing touch football at
the fair grounds.

"Touch football? At this time of night?"

"We had a fluorescent ball," I told her, and I guess
she believed me, because she didn't follow me down to
my dark room in the basement, where I developed the
pictures I'd taken in the cave before I went to bed.

The Triumph of Henry Mulligan

Ever since I started telling these stories people have been wondering what my last name is, and I never tell anyone—for a very good reason. It's Finckledinck! And the only reason I mention it now, is that it was the first thing I heard the next morning when my mother hollered up the stairs, "Charlie Finckledinck! Are you stuck to that mattress?"

There's something about that name that always wakes me up when I hear it. And there's something else about that makes me wish I could stay in bed. But, if I do, my mother's next move is to come upstairs with the kitchen broom and pretend she's sweeping the cobwebs off me. If you've never had a stiff straw broom brushed up and down your backside the first thing in the morning, you've got a lot to look forward to.

Especially if you sleep in the raw, as I do sometimes, when I'm really tired.

Anyway, forget I mentioned my last name, because I won't mention it again, and please don't tell anybody you know what it is.

This morning I didn't wait for the broom treatment. I sprang out of bed like a man jumping out of a snake pit, wondering what time it was and where I'd left my clothes the night before. I stumbled right over a chair, trying to get to the alarm clock on the dresser, and the photographs I'd printed before I went to bed went skidding across the floor. "Jeepers!" I thought. "I bet Jeff and Henry are already at the dock by Jeff's cabin. And they're wondering where I am. I'll tell 'em I was sick with that bug that's going around. No, I'll tell 'em my old man made me mow the lawn. Shucks! Mortimer helped me mow it two days ago. Holy Mackerel!" I grabbed the clock and squinted at it, and it said three-thirty. Then I really panicked!

"Hey, Ma! What time is it?" I hollered from the top of the stairs.

"It's time you were up, young man!"

I should have known better.

"Hey, Ma! It's important. Don't you know what time it is?"

"If you'd get up at a decent hour, you'd know what time it is."

"Please, Ma! What time does the kitchen clock say?"

"I don't know what it says. I'm in the living room. You have a clock in your room! Did you forget to wind it?"

"I don't know. But I hope I did!" And I thumped downstairs stark naked, and dashed through the living room toward the kitchen. I heard a loud scream, and there in front of the refrigerator I saw Mrs. Appleby from next door throwing her hands up over her face, and I just kept going and skidded across the kitchen floor and down behind the stove and grabbed a dishtowel off the rack and threw it around me. Then I cut out for the front stairway again, and by this time Mrs. Appleby was laughing so hard she was all doubled over and red in the face, and I guess I was red all over, too, from top to bottom, and I made it to the top of the stairs in a hop, a step, and a jump.

"What time was it, Charlie?" my mother called after me.

"I don't know," I said. "I forgot to look."

Then I could hear my mother laughing, too, and I felt like a real chump, and I kicked the newel post at the top of the stairs and just about broke my big toe.

"Mrs. Appleby says it's seven-thirty, Charlie, and she wants to know what time the second act comes on."

Mortimer would have had an answer for Mrs. Appleby, but I didn't, so I just stomped into my room and started jumping into my clothes. If I hurried, I'd just have time to make it to the lake. I got my clothes on and grabbed the photos and dashed down the stairs again and out through the kitchen.

"My! Doesn't he look nice with his clothes on," said Mrs. Appleby as I flashed by her.

"Charlie! Where are you going?" screamed my mother. "You haven't had a bite of breakfast." But I was already down the back steps and onto my bike and I pretended I didn't hear her. Mothers always want you to hurry and get out of bed; but if you want to hurry through breakfast, or skip it, the whole world can wait, as far as they're concerned. It's 'You finish your cereal!', and 'Nothing's so important that it can't wait until you have a good breakfast!', and 'You sit right there and eat every bit of that egg, or you don't go at all!', and all that bosh. You'd think the fate of the world rested on two soft-boiled eggs and a piece of toast; or that a bowl of hot cereal would have turned the tide at the battle of Waterloo.

"Charlie Finckledinck, what *are* you up to?" my mother shouted at me as I pedaled down the driveway.

"You wouldn't understand," I shouted back. "It's scientific!"

When I got to the lake, there was already a small crowd of reporters near Jeff's cottage arguing with two Air Policemen and a deputy from the sheriff's office. The police had put up road barriers all along the roadway and I saw Henry and Jeff perched on one of them near Jeff's cottage. Mr. Jenkins was talking to them while his cameraman set up all his equipment to do some filming. Freddy Muldoon was standing to one side with his hands on his hips, watching every move the cameraman made.

"Hey, c'mon, Charlie!" he shouted at me. "You're gonna be on TV!"

"What's up?" I asked Henry. "I got up late, but I got here as fast as I could."

"You're in plenty of time. We have to wait for Chief Putney to get here and settle the argument about whether we can go out on Jeff's dock."

"Did you bring the pictures?"

"They're in my shirt."

"How do they look?" Jeff asked.

"Pretty good. One of them is a *beaut!*"

"Let's see 'em," said Jeff, and he and Henry got

down off the barrier and we went off to one side where nobody could hear us.

"Wow!" said Jeff, when I showed them the shot I'd taken looking down on the bomb from the front end. "That's great, Charlie. That oughta convince 'em." And he waved the photo at Mr. Jenkins, who was standing nearby.

Mr. Jenkins came over, and I hurriedly stuffed the photos back into my shirt.

"That's all right, Charlie," said Henry, holding his hand out. "Let me let have that last shot. I want to let Jenkins take just one peek at it."

"What's that you have there?" Mr. Jenkins asked, as he came up to us.

Henry flashed the photo at him. "What do you think that is?"

"I've no idea. Looks like a tank of bottled gas. Or maybe a wing tank—Hey! That couldn't be an H-bomb, could it? This picture's kinda fuzzy. Where did you get it?"

"You might say we fished it out of the lake," said Henry.

"Henry, is this what you brought us out here to show us?"

"No! I brought you out here to show you *where* the bomb is. Now, if you can talk Chief Putney into letting us go out onto the dock you might have a pretty good story. I think that's him coming now."

Henry stuffed the photo into his own shirt, and we started walking over to the crowd of reporters, where Chief Putney's car and a state police car had just pulled up.

"Hey! I thought we were going to have an interview," the little cameraman shouted. "I just got everything set up."

"Break it down!" Mr. Jenkins said over his shoulder. "It's too late now. We'll try and do it out on the dock."

Chief Putney got out of his car with an Air Force captain following him and a state police sergeant got out of the other car. There was a lot of persiflage and gobbledygook that followed, with everybody standing around and scratching their elbows while Chief Putney tried to figure out what was going on.

"Nobody's allowed out on that lake for any reason," the Air Force captain said to the reporters, "so you might as well go back to your hotels, or wherever you came from."

"Uh...just a minute, Captain Whitehead," Chief Putney interrupted, putting a hand on the captain's shoulder. "I believe the town of Mammoth Falls is still within my jurisdiction. I put the lake and these cottages "off limits" at the request of the Air Force, but I don't remember handing over my badge. Now, gentlemen, if you'll just explain to me what you want to do, then perhaps I can decide whether I can permit it."

"We don't want to go out on the lake, Chief," said Mr. Jenkins, stepping forward. "We just want to go out on that dock and take a few pictures."

"No cameras are permitted in a security area!" said Captain Whitehead.

"Well now..." Chief Putney cleared his throat. "I don't exactly remember anyone declaring this a security area."

"That's what I've been told!...sir!"

"Well somebody must have forgotten to tell *me*. I'm just supposed to keep people off the lake. Nobody ever said anything about pictures."

"These people would have to get permission from

the base, sir."

"Well, Captain Whitehead, you go and check with your headquarters for whatever permission you think *you* need. But, as far as I'm concerned, these gentlemen of the press can go out there and take pictures as long as they convince me they have a legitimate reason."

"We have a reason!" said Mr. Jenkins. "It's simple. The Air Force claims they don't know where the bomb is. These kids claim *they* know where it is, and can prove it if we can just get out on that dock."

"How are they gonna prove it?"

"I don't know! But I'd be stupid if I didn't follow up on a story like this. Confidentially, Chief, they've already shown me enough to make me think they know what they're talking about."

"What did they show you?"

"I'd rather not say."

"Isn't that that Mulligan kid who was getting his hair all tangled up in Congressman Hawkins' fingers yesterday?"

"Yes, that's him."

"Didn't I see him on TV last night?"

"You may have. He was the one trying to get out from under the congressman's arm."

"Oh! Say, he's the one everybody's calling the 'mad scientist', right?"

"Yeah! That's him all right!" said another newsman. "The one with the big map and the 'magnometer' and all that malarkey."

"Well! This I've got to see for myself," said Chief Putney. "Follow me, gentlemen!" And he lifted one of the barriers aside and strode toward the dock.

"Chief Putney, sir!"

"Yes, Captain Whitehead?"

"I must tell you that I'm required to report this to my headquarters!"

"By all means, Captain Whitehead. And don't forget to tell them that these gentlemen sighted some suspicious interlopers on the lake, and they're going to show me where they saw them. Come along, gentlemen!"

With a wink from Chief Putney, and a loud cheer from all the reporters we all moved through the line of barriers and walked out to the dock in front of Jeff's cottage. Mr. Jenkins's cameraman came scrambling along behind us, complaining that he wouldn't have time to get set up, and dropping one piece of equipment or another at every step. Homer and Dinky took pity on him and carried his tripod and film case for him, while he trundled everything else along on a battered wooden dolly.

Harmon Muldoon, of course, had to run out to the end of the dock 'way ahead of everyone else, and was all ready to give one of his speeches when the rest of us got there.

"Step right up, ladies and gentlemen," he chanted, with his lips pressed tightly together, while he beat a tattoo on the dock with a long willow branch he'd been whittling on. "You are about to see one of the most amazing feats of legerdemain ever demonstrated before the crowned heads of Europe. Not only will the internationally famous Dr. Mulligan mystify you with his fantastic feats of memory, but he will also make a liar out of anyone who contradicts him, and once and for all prove that the hand is bigger than the eye!..."

"Knock it off, Harmon! Knock it off!" said Jeff. "Let Henry do the talking."

But Harmon went right on: "Ladies and gentlemen, you will now witness one of the most astounding...." and he fell right off the end of the dock as he made one of his sweeping gestures in the direction of the peninsula.

"Nobody's allowed in the lake!" Chief Putney shouted. "Get out of there, young man!"

But Harmon couldn't hear him. He was four feet under, on the bottom, and only his sailor cap and the willow branch were visible, floating on the surface. When he came up, two of the reporters helped us pull him up onto the dock and Mortimer slapped his sopping wet hat back on his head.

"We oughta revoke your club privileges for conduct unbecoming a scientist," he said. "Now, run up and down the dock till you dry up!"

The reporters were all laughing at Harmon, but Harmon wasn't laughing. He stomped up and down the dock, cursing to himself and blaming everything imaginable for the fact he had fallen in the water. Chief Putney told him to stay at the beach end of the dock, and he herded the reporters together at the other end.

"And now, 'Dr. Mulligan'," he said. "Just what is it you brought us out here for?"

Henry stood at the extreme end of the dock and pointed out toward the peninsula. "If you'll all get your cameras focused on the nose of that peninsula, we're prepared to show you that we know where the bomb is located. Just let me know when you're ready."

"Can you give us some idea of what we're going to photograph?" asked one cameraman. "I'd like to be all set."

"It'll be a bright orange object," said Henry.

"Where is it? I don't see any bright orange object

out there."

"I don't either," said Henry. "If I did, I'd be a little worried."

"What does that mean, wise guy?"

"It means there isn't any bright orange object out there right now, but there will be when you're ready."

"I guess that skinny kid that fell in the water was right," said one of the reporters out of the side of his mouth. "This looks more like a sideshow every minute."

"Yeah!" said another wisecracker. "This may be the greatest stunt since Moses parted the waters of the Red Sea. I bet this kid's gonna make the lake open up so we can get a picture of the bomb right on the bottom!"

Everybody laughed at that one, and you could see Henry's ears starting to stick out a little bit, and his scalp jerked back and forth a couple of times.

"Is everybody ready?" Henry asked, rather hesitantly.

"I'm ready, and I guess that means everybody is," said the little cameraman with Mr. Jenkins.

A big cheer went up from the other photographers. "You wouldn't kid us, would you Shorty?" "Hey, everybody! Shorty's ready!" "Okay, Dr. Mulligan! Shorty says you can start the miracle!" For some reason, everybody called him "Shorty," but I don't think that was his real name.

Henry walked to the edge of the dock and Jeff handed him a black gadget with a lot of buttons on it. Henry pointed the gadget toward the distant peninsula, looked back at the photographers to see if they were ready, then raised his left hand dramatically and pushed one of the buttons.

Nothing happened.

There was a long pause that got a little embarrassing. The photographers kept looking through their view-finders, then looking at Henry, then looking through their view-finders again.

Still, nothing happened.

Henry pushed the button again, and then shaded his eyes from the sun to look out toward the peninsula. I strained my eyes, but there was nothing to be seen but water. Something was wrong!

Jeff stepped over to Henry, while the photographers and reporters started mumbling to each other and making wisecracks again. "Henry!" he said in a low voice. "Don't tell me you turned that receiver off instead of turning it on last night?"

"I'm sure I turned it on," said Henry. "Maybe it got wet."

"Try it again!"

Henry pushed the button again, but nothing happened for the third time.

"Hey, you got a no-hitter going, kiddo! Hang in there, boy!" one of the photographers shouted.

Henry flushed red, right up to the roots of his hair, and turned his back on the reporters. "It's okay, fellas," he said hoarsely. "I just forgot to turn on the transmitter, that's all." And he flicked a switch on the black gadget.

I heaved a sigh of relief. And, then, I busted out laughing. I just couldn't help it. Henry looked at me as if I'd just told him his best girlfriend was dating my older brother—except Henry never has any girlfriends and I don't have any older brother. Then he turned toward the reporters and pointed at the peninsula again, and pushed the button.

"Hey, look! Hey, look!" one of the photographers shouted, and they all started looking through their view-finders again, and there was a lot of shutter-snapping going on.

Far out on the lake, about three hundred yards west of the peninsula, something bright and orange started bulging out of the water until it grew to about the size of a five hundred-pound turnip. Then it started rising above the water, and growing even bigger as it gained altitude above the surface of the lake. At about a hundred feet it came up short with a jerk and bobbed up and down a bit until it settled down and floated there, swaying gently from side to side.

Another cheer went up from the group of reporters and photographers. And this time it was a real loud one with a different tone to it. "Attaboy, Mulligan!" "Go get 'em, Dr. Mulligan!" "Hey! What is that? An atom's apple, maybe?" So many questions were being thrown at Henry that Chief Putney had to step forward and save him from being pushed right off the end of the dock.

"One at a time, gentlemen, one at a time, if you don't mind," said the chief. "Now, young Mulligan. Would you mind telling me just what that is out there, and what it has to do with the bomb?"

"That's a weather balloon," Henry explained. "And it's anchored to the spot where the bomb is located. If you'll get the Air Force to send their divers down to the end of that line, they'll find the bomb there."

"Holy Mackerel! Is this for real, kid?" one of the reporters asked.

"You sure you aren't just putting on a sideshow for us?" asked another.

"How did that balloon get out there, anyway?"

"We put it out there last night," said Henry. "Just after we found the bomb."

"Just after you found the bomb?"

"Yes!" said Henry. "I told you yesterday we knew where the bomb was, and you asked me to prove it. There's the proof, right there!" And Henry pointed toward the orange balloon.

"But that's just a balloon!"

"We've got more proof, if you need it," said Jeff. "But all you have to do is get the Air Force to send divers down to the end of that line the balloon is tied to, and they'll find the bomb."

"Hey, Dr. Mulligan!" one of the cameramen said loudly. "Can you bring that balloon back down and send it up again? I'm not sure I got a good picture."

There was a lot of snickering in the crowd of cameramen, and one of them nudged the man next to him. "There goes old 'Flash' Fitzgerald again. He never gets the shot the first time."

"Yeah, he'd have asked for a replay of the Hindenburg disaster, if he'd been there," said the other.

"That's why they never send him out when somebody's threatening to jump off a building," said another man. "I remember one time he missed the shot and he offered a bystander fifty bucks to re-enact the jump!"

"It's just a one-shot system," Henry explained to the cameraman. "We can send the balloon up once. But we can't bring it back down again."

"All kidding aside, Henry," said Mr. Jenkins, pulling Henry off to one side. "How *did* you get that balloon out there, and how did you get it to go up just when you wanted it to?"

"It's simple," said Henry. Then he gulped. "That is, if you don't forget to turn on the juice. Have you ever been to a model airplane meet where they fly radio-controlled planes?"

"No! But I've read about them."

"Well, you probably know that you have a transmitter on the ground, and a receiver in the airplane. You can send signals to the plane and make it turn right or left, slow down, speed up...or anything you want."

"Yeah! I know that."

"Well, this is a transmitter," said Henry, holding up the black gadget with all the buttons on it. "Out there, on the lake, we have the receiver mounted on a float that we rigged up last night. We used it to puncture the capsule that inflated the balloon. That's all there is to it."

"Except you have to remember to turn on the juice," added Mortimer.

"Very ingenious!" said Chief Putney.

"Now you know why I'm beginning to believe these kids," said Mr. Jenkins.

"You're starting to make a convert out of me, too. But there's just one thing that puzzles me. I can see that balloon. But how do I know there's a bomb at the end of that line?"

"What about that, Henry?"

"We can prove the bomb is there, if it's necessary," said Henry.

"You mean that picture you showed me?" said Mr. Jenkins.

"Yes."

"Well...assuming it is a picture of an H-bomb...."

Well...how do I know where you got that picture? Henry, I just can't believe that you actually took a picture of a bomb the Air Force hasn't been able to find for three days."

"There's something about that picture you didn't notice, Mr. Jenkins."

"What's that?"

"Never mind," said Henry, looking out toward the balloon to hide a mischievous smile that had come over his face. "I'll let you know when the time comes."

"Why can't you tell me now?"

"I could, but I don't want to. My father always says you don't blow your trump card till you have to, and I believe him!"

"Okay, Dr. Mulligan!" Mr. Jenkins said with a smile. "I'll take your word for it." Then his brow puckered a bit. "I suppose what you want us to do now is challenge the Air Force to send some divers down there where the balloon is."

"Can you think of a better way to find out if it's there?" said Henry. "Of course, if you know how to skin dive, we could take you out there tonight, and you could see for yourself."

"No thanks!" said Mr. Jenkins, and all the reporters started laughing and kidding him. "I'm sure Chief Putney would throw me in jail if I did that." Then he turned toward the other reporters, "I say let's go and put it up to the Air Force! Let's get out to the air base."

There was a big cheer, and everybody started moving off the dock, but Mr. Jenkins stopped us and said, "Just for Shorty's sake, could we do an interview right here, while we've got that balloon in the background?"

Henry shrugged his shoulders and looked at Jeff,

and Jeff shrugged his shoulders and looked at the rest of us, and Harmon said, "Heck, yes! I can't think of a better place. Besides, I'm still wet, so I'll look as if I just came up out of the drink."

"Must have been pretty strong drink!" said Mortimer, holding his nose.

So we all stayed and posed for Mr. Jenkins while he asked Henry and Jeff a lot of stupid questions about how we found the bomb, and how come we didn't get caught by the police while we were out on the lake, and a lot of junk like that. We let Harmon explain how we got around the two patrol cars where the tracks cross Turkey Hill Road; but when we watched the news on TV that night, that part got cut out for a commercial announcement and Harmon was pretty sore about the whole thing.

The rest of the reporters had disappeared by the time we got finished, and Mr. Jenkins suddenly realized they were probably heading for Westport Field to interview Colonel March, and if he didn't hurry he'd miss out on the story.

"If you don't mind my buttin' in, I don't think Colonel March is at the base," said Chief Putney. "He was due at the Town Hall to meet with the Town Council about the time I got called out here."

"Thanks!" said Mr. Jenkins. "Maybe I can beat the rest of them to it. Mind if I ride back into town with you?"

"If you don't mind people thinking you're under arrest."

"I think I can live it down. Hey, Shorty! Load that stuff in the station wagon and meet me at the Town Hall." Then Mr. Jenkins drove off with Chief Putney, leaving Shorty with all his paraphernalia at the end of the dock.

We got on our bikes and took off for the town square. I had the feeling that something exciting would finally happen, and I could tell the rest of the gang did, too. Everybody was bent over the handlebars, pedaling like blazes, and nobody was doing any talking.

By the time we got there, a huge truck loaded with watermelons was blocking traffic right in front of the Town Hall. Constable Billy Dahr was in the middle of the street arguing with the truck driver, but apparently not winning the argument. And it was a cinch he wouldn't. The driver just happened to be Jaspar Okeby, who is about as cantankerous a character as we have in Mammoth Falls. He runs a pretty good truck garden farm just outside of town on the White Fork Road, and he isn't famous for taking any lip from anybody. Constable Billy Dahr was having a hard time convincing him that he couldn't block the street in front of the Town Hall forever, with traffic piling up behind him.

"I ain't blockin' traffic!" said Jaspar. "I'm jest waitin' fer that car to pull away from the curb, so's I kin back in there and make a delivery." And he pointed to a car standing at the curb with its engine running. Behind it were parked three Air Force sedans that we figured must have brought Colonel March and his staff to the meeting with the Town Council. The first one was certainly Colonel March's, because it had a blue plate above the front bumper with chicken wings on it.

"*Delivery?*" said Billy Dahr. "You can't make a delivery here! Besides, there ain't nobody at the Town Hall ordered any watermelons. What in tarnation are you talkin' about, Jaspar?"

"You ain't in the watermelon business, Billy Dahr, you're in the police business," said Jaspar Okeby. "So how come you know so much about it?"

"I'll show you some police business if you don't move this truck out of here!" said Billy Dahr, shaking his stick at the window of the truck.

"If you're so all-fired smart, why don't you go out and find that consarned bomb they're lookin' fer, so's we can live in peace around here?" said Jaspar, getting all red in the face.

"If I could, I'd dump it in your outhouse for sure!" said Billy Dahr.

While the argument was going on, a man came running out of the Town Hall with a tray full of coffee cups and drove off in the car that had been standing at the curb. Jaspar put his truck in gear and started maneuvering it into the vacant space, while Billy Dahr directed traffic around him.

"Why in tarnation couldn't you park down the street a ways?" he grumbled. "There's plenty a spaces right down there."

"I told you, you ain't in the watermelon business, Billy Dahr, so mind your own business." And Jaspar pulled into the curb and then backed it to within a foot of the front bumper of Colonel March's sedan. An airman sitting in the driver's seat got out and walked up to the door of Jaspar's truck.

"How about pulling it up a bit, so I can get out, Buddy? The Colonel will be comin' out any minute now."

"That's fine by me," said Jaspar. "Matter of fact I'll jest be here a minute. Now stand back, Sonny...unless you're danged fond of watermelon!"

And with that, Jaspar revved up the motor of his

truck, and the dump body started tilting upward and watermelons came cascading off the top of the load and plummeting onto the hood of Colonel March's sedan.

"Hey! Hey! What are you doing, you old fool?" the airman shouted. "Stop it! Stop it! You're dumping your load!"

"I know it!" said Jaspar. "Jest wait'll I get her all the way up!"

"Hey! You're dumpin' right on the Colonel's car." And the airman dashed to the door of the sedan to try and open it. But he thought better of the matter when melons started bouncing off the roof and thumping onto the sidewalk and street. By this time the torrent of melons plumping onto the roof of the car sounded like the rumble of thunder, and people came running out of all the stores and eating places around the square to see what all the commotion was about. Kids materialized out of nowhere, like worms coming out of the woodwork, and they came scrambling across the square to grab the watermelons that popped open as they hit the pavement. Billy Dahr had halted all the traffic in both directions and was jumping up and down in the middle of the street, waving his stick in the air.

"Jaspar! Consarn it! You're losing all your melons!" he shouted.

"Ain't that a shame!" Jaspar shouted back.

The dump body kept going up and the watermelons kept tumbling out of it until there was a heap of them ten feet high standing in front of the Town Hall and Colonel March's car had completely disappeared somewhere under the pile. Then Jaspar pulled his truck forward, letting the last few melons trickle out onto the street, and started to lower the body. The airman stood there in the middle of the street with his hands on his hips, shaking his head slowly back and forth. And Billy Dahr hoisted himself onto the running board of the truck and shook his stick in Jaspar's face.

"Jaspar Okeby, I'm placing you under arrest for destroying government property."

"You can't arrest me, Billy Dahr. I ain't destroyed nothin'," said Jaspar, pushing his hand in Billy Dahr's moustache as he got out of his truck.

"I'm jest deliverin' some melons, like I told you." His face wasn't red anymore. It was positively vermilion.

"I warn you! Anything you say may be held against you."

"And I warn you, Billy Dahr! Don't say nothin' to make me mad, or I might do somethin' stupid that I'd be sorry for."

"I'd hate to see Jaspar when he was really mad," said a bystander.

By now, a big crowd had gathered to listen to the argument, and a lot of people were just milling around the pile of watermelons, kicking at them with their toes and looking over their shoulders as if they wondered whether they couldn't just pick one up and walk off with it. But the kids weren't wondering about anything. They were just grabbing melons as fast as they could and lugging them off to a place on the grass where they could sit down and get their ears wet eating them.

Billy Dahr's moustache was jumping up and down, and you could hear his false teeth clacking as he tried to decide what to say next.

"Jaspar Okeby, if you don't wanna go to jail, you just up and get them melons outa here! I tol' you, you couldn't make no delivery here!"

"Them ain't my melons," said Jaspar. "They're the colonel's melons. Let him get 'em outa here."

"What's the matter with you, you old fossil-head?" said the airman. "The colonel didn't order no melons. Leastways, he didn't order 'em delivered here."

"I didn't say he ordered 'em, young fella. Them melons is a present. No charge! And I got three or four more loads to bring him, 'fore I'm finished."

"Is this old guy a nut?" said the airman, turning to Billy Dahr. "Look at the colonel's car. You can't even see it!"

"That's fer dang sure!" said Billy Dahr.

Just then Chief Putney came striding down the steps of the Town Hall with Mr. Jenkins following him, and at the same time three cars came wheeling into the square from Vesey Street and the mob of reporters that had gone out to the air base jumped out of them and came running across the park. Chief Putney stopped in mid-stride when he saw the huge mound of melons, and scratched his head. Then he came trotting up to Billy Dahr.

"What's going on here, Constable Dahr?"

"I don't rightly know, Chief," said Billy.

"I can tell you what's going on," said the airman. "Look at Colonel March's car!"

"Looks all right to me," said Chief Putney. "Which one is it?"

"That's what's the matter with it," said the airman. "You can't see it! It's the one under the watermelons."

"Under the watermelons? Constable Dahr! Is there a car under those watermelons?"

"There was about two minutes ago, Chief, but right now I wouldn't be sure of anything. It's the dad-blamedest thing I ever did see. I jest don't know what this town is comin' to."

"Well, what are all these melons doing here, anyway? Who dumped them here?"

"Jaspar Okeby done it," said Constable Dahr, gesturing toward Jaspar's truck. "I tol' him not to do it, but he went ahead and done it anyway."

Chief Putney walked slowly over to the truck, where Jaspar was fastening down his dump body.

"I'm gonna ask you just one question, Jaspar Okeby! And I want a straight answer."

"You don't have to ask me no questions," said Jaspar, getting red in the face again. "You wanna know who dumped them melons. Well, this here's a dump truck, and it has my name on it, and you know I raise melons, and I don't see no other dump trucks around here, right at present. Now, you bein' the chief of the whole police force, and all that, right now you got a first-class opportunity to do some downright brilliant detective work. And I'll give you another hint. If you'll look inside this here body that I'm hitchin' down after jest havin' raised it, you might find a squashed melon or two on the bed."

Chief Putney had been standing there, rocking back and forth on his heels during Jaspar's monologue.

"That isn't the question I wanted to ask you," he said. "All I want to know is *why? Why* did you dump a whole load of melons on the colonel's car?"

Jaspar stuck his thumbs in the straps of his overalls and leaned back against his truck.

"You ever been in the melon business, Harold?"

"You know danged well I've never been in the melon business, Jaspar."

"Then you wouldn't know nothin' about gettin' up at four o'clock in the mornin' to get a load of melons over to the market at Clinton, and then havin' them tell you they ain't buyin' no melons from Mammoth Falls 'cause everything that grows here is contaminated and they can't sell it 'cause nobody will eat anything that comes from Mammoth Falls and you can just take your load back where it came from and let the people in Mammoth Falls eat it. I know you wouldn't know nothin' about that, 'cause you ain't in the melon business. Anyways, I figured that if anybody oughta eat these here melons it oughta be the Air Force, 'cause they know all about atom bombs and all that stuff and they're probably used to eatin' food that's been contaminated, and so I tried to deliver 'em out there to the air base, but they wouldn't let me in the gate, so I brought 'em here and the only parking place I could get into just happened to be right in front of the colonel's fancy see-dan and I guess it's somewhere under that pile right now, if anybody's lookin' for it. And that's all I know about them consarned melons, so there! 'Ceptin' you ought to be glad you're in the police business and not in the melon business!"

"Hot dang! Will you get a load of this character," said one of the reporters. "Hey, Jaspar! Would you mind moving over in front of that pile of melons while we get a few shots?"

Then the reporters took over, and for a while Chief Putney lost control of the situation. Jaspar Okeby was getting peppered with questions so fast he didn't have time to answer any of them, and the photographers were practically manhandling him as they tried to get him to climb up on top of the pile of melons while they took pictures. During all the commotion, the meeting in the Town Hall broke up, and Colonel March came down the steps with several other Air Force officers.

"Hey, Colonel! Would you mind posing for a few pictures in front of that pile of melons?" a photographer shouted at him.

"What for? What is this? Where is my driver? What happened to my car?" the colonel asked.

"Your car is under that pile of melons, Colonel," said one of the reporters. "Some character dumped his load right on it. He claims he couldn't sell his melons because they're contaminated, so he's giving them all to you. Do you have any statement to make, Colonel March?"

"Just a moment, gentlemen," said Lieutenant Graham, stepping forward from the group of officers. "The colonel will have a statement to make just as soon as we have ascertained all the facts."

Then he led the colonel aside, where they conferred for a moment and then motioned to Chief Putney to join them. After a minute, Chief Putney beckoned to Billy Dahr who went over and gestured extravagantly while he described what had taken place, and then bobbed his moustache up and down in agreement with everything that Chief Putney added. The colonel kept looking back over his shoulder at the pile of melons, and shaking his head in disbelief. Then he held a whispered consultation with Lieutenant Graham and nodded his head up and down several times.

"Gentlemen," said the colonel, as he returned to the group of reporters, "I understand that I have been presented with a rather handsome gift from a local citizen."

There was a big laugh, and a lot of people in the crowd surrounding the reporters started making wisecracks like: "You can say that again, Colonel!" and "With friends like you got, who needs enemies?" and "You sure them melons wasn't dropped from an airplane, Colonel?"

"I also understand that the gentleman who left these melons here is very concerned about the possible contamination of his crop," the colonel continued. "I can understand that concern. We have all been through a very trying time. And we aren't out of the woods yet. We haven't found the bomb. And until we do find it, and remove it from your community, I know that many of you will spend sleepless nights and anxious days."

When the colonel mentioned the word *contamination*, a lot of the people who had been standing around with a watermelon under their coats sort of let them slip down onto the ground again when they thought nobody was looking. One man went over to the kids who were sitting cross-legged under the trees slurping melon as fast as they could, and tried to take it away from them. All he got for his trouble was a big, fat raspberry, and a piece of melon behind the ear.

"I want to emphasize once again," the colonel went on, "that there is absolutely no evidence of radiological contamination in this area—at present. You can rest assured that your water is safe to drink, and that the fruit and vegetables grown in this area are safe to eat— regardless of what you may have heard to the contrary. Meanwhile, we are continuing intensive efforts to locate and remove the strategic weapon that was lost. Now, I've been told you should never put a gift horse in your mouth...but I just can't resist the temptation."

Then the colonel brought out a jackknife and picked up the largest and ripest melon he could find. He flicked open the knife and proceeded to cut the melon into segments. He cut a big juicy slice from the center and started gnawing on it as if he was playing a harmonica.

"My, that is delicious!" he said.

Flashbulbs were popping off all over the place as the photographers started shooting pictures. The colonel walked over to where his staff officers were standing and started handing out slices of watermelon. Lieutenant Graham bit off a big mouthful right away, and agreed with the colonel that it was delicious. But some of the other officers made wry faces and looked at each other as if they weren't so sure.

"Take a piece!" said the colonel. "You'll enjoy it!"

Faced with a choice between possible death and disobeying the colonel, they all chose death and sank their teeth into the chunk the colonel handed them.

Some of the people in the crowd started clapping their hands, and there were a few cheers here and there. Colonel March picked up another melon, split it open, and began offering pieces to the newsmen and all the bystanders. A couple of other men in the crowd pulled knives out of their pockets, and pretty soon it seemed as though everybody was either cutting open a watermelon or lugging one home with him. Freddy Muldoon and Dinky Poore lost no time getting their share, but the rest of us didn't feel like munching watermelon right then. We were more interested in whether Mr. Jenkins could buttonhole the colonel and pop the big question to him. So we just stood there and watched the mound of melons slowly disappear until the car had been completely uncovered, and we all had to admit the colonel had made a pretty good move.

While the photographers were still taking pictures of the colonel with his face half-buried in a big piece of melon, Mr. Jenkins and the other reporters started throwing questions at him:

"Any new leads on the bomb, Colonel?"

"Colonel, can we quote you on that statement about no danger of radiation in the area? Is that for certain?"

"Have you definitely eliminated the lake as a possibility, Colonel?"

"Colonel, can you give us some idea of your plans for the immediate future? Where is the search concentrated now?"

The colonel waved off the questions good-naturedly, pulled out his handkerchief, and wiped his mouth. "Gentlemen, I'd like to help you, but the fact is I have absolutely no news for you right now."

"Well, we may have some news for *you*, Colonel," said Mr. Jenkins. "We have good reason to believe the bomb has been located!"

"I can assure you we have *not* located the bomb, gentlemen."

"We know *you* ain't found it, Colonel," said the reporter that always had his coat slung over his arm. "But we've been told it's been found. And, what's more, we know where it is!"

"You know where it is?"

"Let's say we *think* we know where it is," cautioned Mr. Jenkins. "What we want you to do, Colonel, is prove to us, once and for all, whether or not these kids know what they're talking about."

"What are you saying? What kids? Oh! That's the young man who was here yesterday with the map, isn't it?"

"Yes!"

"I already told you gentlemen we had searched that part of the lake thoroughly. I have nothing to add to that statement."

"Uh, just a minute, Colonel," said another reporter, shifting a big cigar from one side of his mouth to the other. "Out there on that lake we just saw a great big orange balloon come up out of the water when nobody was within a mile of it. This kid here made it come up with some kind of radio gadget and a lot of hocus-pocus. He claims that balloon is anchored right where the bomb is. After what I saw this morning, I gotta believe him unless you can prove he's wrong! In other words, Colonel, if you don't check this out, my paper's gonna print a story about how these kids know where the bomb is and the Air Force refuses to do anything about it."

"Wait a minute!" Lieutenant Graham interrupted, "That's not exactly what the colonel said."

"That's what I'm hearing," said the reporter. "I don't care what words he's usin'."

"What's all this about a big orange balloon?" asked the colonel.

"Go down to the lake and see for yourself," said the reporter. "It's still there."

"Is this some kind of a prank?" the colonel asked. "The lake has been 'off limits' for three days. How could anyone anchor a balloon out there?"

"I don't know how they did it, or when they did it," said the reporter, "but there's a balloon out there right now, and these kids say if you'll send some divers down to the end of that line, you'll find the bomb. Now, what are you going to do about it, Colonel?"

"Well!" said the colonel. "I haven't seen the balloon,

but I'll take your word for it that it's there. But that doesn't prove anything. I don't plan to do anything unless somebody can show me some evidence that justifies sending divers down in that part of the lake again."

"Thank you all, gentlemen," said Lieutenant Graham, stepping into the breach. "If you will keep in touch with my office, we will let you know as soon as there is any new development."

There was some grumbling among the reporters as Lieutenant Graham started to escort Colonel March toward his car, and Shorty the cameraman slipped on a juicy watermelon rind and fell flat on his right ear as he was trying to get into position to film the colonel getting into his sedan. It was then that Henry plucked at Mr. Jenkins's elbow and pulled the photo out of his shirt.

"Just a moment, Lieutenant," said Mr. Jenkins. "I have something here that I think the colonel should see." And he took the photo from Henry and held it up in front of Colonel March.

"What is that?" the colonel asked.

"That's what I want you to tell *me*, Colonel. Is that an H-bomb?"

"It certainly looks like one...but," the colonel hesitated..."this is a pretty murky picture."

"It was taken underwater," Mr. Jenkins explained.

"That picture is classified!" said Lieutenant Graham, peering over the colonel's shoulder. "Where did you get it?"

"Never mind where I got it. *Is* that an H-bomb?"

Several of the other officers peeked over the colonel's shoulder to look at the photo, and then stared at each other in amazement.

"Well, Mr. Jenkins," the colonel said slowly, "if that isn't an H-bomb, it's a very good imitation of one. But I would like to know where you got this photo."

"I can't tell you that, colonel. But I'm told that this photo was taken last night out in Strawberry Lake."

The colonel snorted and several of his officers laughed outright.

"You're not seriously asking me to believe such a story, are you, Mr. Jenkins? I don't know where you got that photograph, but it appears to be a photo of a nuclear device...and it probably is classified information, as Lieutenant Graham suggests. I think you should turn it over to my staff and let them make an investigation to determine where it came from."

Lieutenant Graham reached out to take the photo, but Mr. Jenkins pulled it back out of reach.

"Not so fast, Lieutenant. This picture doesn't belong to you!"

"Frankly, Mr. Jenkins, I think somebody has been pulling your leg," said the colonel. "That picture has probably been copied from some Air Force manual, and if you'll just hand it over to Lieutenant Graham, we'll try and find out where it came from. I think you're being victimized by someone who's trying to pass that off as a picture of the bomb that was lost. It's a very clever stunt, but we don't have time for clever stunts just now. We have a serious problem on our hands, and it demands all our attention."

"Could you repeat that, Colonel?" several reporters asked. "Can we get that on tape, Colonel?" said a couple of others. And suddenly there were four microphones thrust in front of the colonel's face.

While this was going on, Mr. Jenkins felt somebody

plucking at his sleeve again, and he turned to find Henry offering him a small magnifying glass.

"I told you there was something about that picture you hadn't noticed, Mr. Jenkins," said Henry. "Take a close look, right where my finger is."

Mr. Jenkins squinted through the magnifying glass. Then his face lit up. "Looks like some kind of a number," he said. "And there's a whole bunch of gobbledy-gook letters, too! Is this your trump card, Henry?"

"If you want to see them really flip their lids, get the colonel to read that number. And if it turns out to be a serial number, like I think it is, how about buying hamburgers for the whole gang? We're getting hungry."

"You're on!" said Mr. Jenkins, and he strode over to where the other reporters were taping Colonel March's statement. "Colonel March, sir! Before you go on record with that statement, I think you ought to take a closer look at this photograph." Then he looked at Lieutenant Graham with a broad grin. "I just don't think it's fair to expect the colonel to make a statement until he has had a chance to ascertain all the facts."

Lieutenant Graham looked a little sheepish as he nodded his head, but Colonel March was somewhat annoyed at the interruption and he looked at Mr. Jenkins with an air of exasperation.

"What is it now?" he asked, rather curtly.

"I just think you ought to take a close look at this photograph...right here," and pointed with his finger as he held the photo up.

The colonel squinted with one eye through the magnifying glass, then he looked up at Mr. Jenkins, then he peered through the glass with the other eye. Then he looked up again, and his eyes were bugging out.

"Richardson!" he roared. "Take a look at this picture!"

A harassed-looking major stepped forward briskly and scrutinized the photo carefully, in the area where the colonel was holding his finger.

"Is that the number of the weapon we're looking for, or isn't it?"

The major hastily pulled a small notebook from his breast pocket and fingered through the pages. Then he looked carefully at the photo again.

"I don't understand it," he said. "I don't understand it. It can't be!"

"Well, is it the number, or isn't it?"

"It is!" said the major, nodding his head. "But I don't understand it. How could anyone have gotten a picture of it?"

"There seems to be a lot going on that we don't understand," said the colonel. "Mr. Jenkins! It seems to me that you have a lot of explaining to do. I ask you again: *Where* did you get this photo?"

"I told you I can't tell you that," said Mr. Jenkins.

"Pardon me, Colonel," said the reporter with the big cigar, pushing his broad frame into the tight circle that had gathered around the colonel and Mr. Jenkins, "but it seems to me that *you're* the one that has a lot of explaining to do. Now...."

"Where is the negative of that photo?" the major named Richardson demanded. "You said it was taken out on the lake last night. Somebody has the negative, and I demand that you produce it. That's classified information!"

"Just a minute, buster!" said the big reporter, jabbing his finger right under the major's nose. "I believe I was asking the colonel a very important question just now, and you interrupted me. Now you're just gonna step back and keep out of this until I have an answer from the colonel!"

"Lieutenant Graham, I think this is getting a bit out of hand," said the colonel.

"Yes, sir!" the lieutenant agreed.

"Now, as I was saying," the big reporter continued, "I think you're the one that has some explaining to do, Colonel. These kids here have been trying to tell you that they know where that bomb is ever since yesterday morning. Now, I'll admit that I didn't believe them, either. But this morning I saw a big orange balloon come up out of nowhere, and now I see a photograph of a bomb that your own officer admits has the right serial number on it. And all you seem to be worried about is where the photograph came from. Now let me give you some advice, Colonel. If you want to get your nose rubbed in printers ink all over this country, you just keep on harassin' Mr. Jenkins here about where that photo came from. But it might interest you to know that my editor doesn't give a hoot about that photo. What he will want to know is *just what you plan to do about recovering that bomb!* So, supposing you just tell us, in twenty-five words or less, what your immediate plans are!"

"We plan to send divers down immediately, in the area where that balloon is anchored!" said the colonel, fixing a furious eye on Major Richardson.

"And just when is *immediately*, Colonel?"

"This afternoon!"

"Thank you, Colonel. I think I can go file a story, now."

And the big reporter turned away, as a rousing cheer went up from the rest of the newsmen and the hangers-on left over from the watermelon feast.

"Thanks for helping me out, Mac!" Mr. Jenkins said to the big man. "The colonel had me on a spot there, and I didn't want to press him too much."

"Any time, Jake! I don't mind pressing 'em. Sometimes it takes some of the starch out of 'em."

"By the way, Mac, have you met 'Professor' Mulligan? Henry! This is Earl MacComber. He's covering the story for the Associated Press."

"*Professor?* I thought it was Doctor Mulligan! I'll have to send a correction in to the office," said Mr. MacComber, with a big, belly-rumbler of a laugh. "Very nice to meet you formally, sonny." Then he grabbed Henry's skinny hand with one giant paw and Henry went right down on one knee as he squealed, "Very nice to meet you, too, sir!"

"You kids are putting on a great show, sonny," Mr. MacComber went on, "but now we come to the moment of truth. We'll soon know whether you've been pulling our leg."

And he strutted off across the park toward the Bristol Hotel to phone his story in.

The Sword
of Damocles

As soon as Mr. MacComber had left, Mr. Jenkins button-holed the colonel to get him to repeat his statement for the TV camera, and the reporters with the tape recorders got in on the act, too. Meanwhile, the crowd in the town square practically evaporated. Everybody seemed to want to get home, or to a telephone, and spread the latest news as fast as they could. About all that was left was a crew of firemen that Constable Dahr had brought over from the fire house to hose down the sidewalks and clean up the mess left over from the watermelon debacle.

Harmon Muldoon tried to make their job as easy as possible by starting a game of melon-in-the-ear with two friends of his that had turned up in the crowd. They kept dodging in and out among the trees, throwing big, juicy hunks of watermelon rind at each other, until one of them finally knocked the helmet right off a fireman's head with a big chunk. His name was Stony Martin, and he started laughing like a hyena when he saw the helmet hit the ground, but he forgot to keep his eyes open. Two of the other firemen aimed the high-pressure hose at him and knocked him flat on the grass.

Stony struggled back to his feet, with the breath knocked half out of him, and he and his friend took off across the square like two scared rabbits.

"Are those some of the kids that claim they found the lost bomb?" Colonel March asked.

"I don't know who they are, Colonel. I never saw them before," said Mr. Jenkins.

Harmon came sauntering back toward us, with his thumbs stuck in his trouser pockets, and a big, fat grin on his face.

"Get out of here, Harmon!" Jeff bit the words off out of the side of his mouth. "And don't *ever* come back!"

The grin faded from Harmon's face. He started to bluster, and the thumbs came out of his pockets to form two fists. But when he saw the angry glare in Jeff's eyes, he put his hands back in his pockets and contented himself with a loud, juicy raspberry that spattered a couple of watermelon seeds on my arm. Then he turned on his heel and waddled off toward Vesey Street. And he never did come back—except to haunt us.

As Colonel March started toward his car he stopped in front of Jeff and Henry.

"You know...something puzzles me, Richardson," he said to the major who was hovering at his shoulder. "You claim our divers searched the lake bottom thoroughly, all along the line of flight...and they're supposed to be professional divers. If these kids *did* find the bomb—and I still don't know *how* they did—how come your divers missed it?"

The major gulped noticeably.

"It's very, very deep right in that area, sir! Maybe two hundred feet!"

"I don't care how deep it is. The point is, *did* they search the bottom?"

"The bomb's not on the bottom, sir," Jeff volunteered. "It's in a cave."

"In a *cave?*"

"Yes, sir!"

"You see, sir," Henry explained, "there's an underwater ridge that runs out into the lake right off the nose of that peninsula. It isn't very wide, but it runs out into the lake quite a distance, and about three hundred yards out, it's still only thirty feet or so under the surface. Right there is where our magnetometer registered a big deviation in the magnetic field, and we found this cave about another twenty feet down the south slope of that ridge."

"You can't see the cave at first," Jeff added, "because the mouth is all covered with tall weeds. But, if you'll just have your divers go right down the line that balloon is tied to, they'll find my anchor right at the entrance."

"And watch out for them trout!" said Freddy Muldoon. "Charlie says there's some real big ones in there."

The colonel smiled. Then his face got very stern.

"Just how did you kids get out on that lake to do all this? If you *did* do it?"

"That's classified information," said Mortimer, quickly,

and even Major Richardson managed a snickering kind of a laugh.

"Well, gentlemen, I'll take that up with you later," said the colonel, looking very serious again. "Right now we've got a lot of work to do." And he started toward his car.

A few reporters were still hanging around, and they kept badgering the colonel as he was getting into his car about whether they could go along with the divers and observe the recovery operations. But the colonel just kept shaking his head.

"Absolutely not!" he said. "Not only is this a classified device we're looking for, but I just cannot be responsible for any possible injury to a civilian. It's just too dangerous."

"You mean this thing might still go off, Colonel?"

"The colonel didn't say that!" Lieutenant Graham interjected.

"These devices are not armed on training flights," the colonel explained. "They would only be armed in the event of an actual tactical mission flown in a national emergency...and even then, only when the flight had reached the target area. I thought I had already explained all that. But these weapons also carry a conventional explosive that is detonated to trigger the nuclear device. It is the conventional explosives that I am worried about. You just can't take too many precautions when you're handling ordnance items of any kind."

"Does that make the situation clear to you gentlemen?" Lieutenant Graham asked.

There was a little grumbling, but the newsmen nodded their heads and the three Air Force sedans pulled away from the curb with their tires spinning a little. There was still some melon rind and slippery goo left in the street, and Colonel March's car looked pretty wet and sticky, but I imagine it got a good bath as soon as it got back to the air base.

As the cars drove out of sight, Henry looked up at Mr. Jenkins, and Mr. Jenkins started counting noses.

"I think I owe you all a hamburger. Let's see...four, six, seven. I thought there were eight of you. What happened to the kid that fell in the lake?"

"He never came up," said Freddy Muldoon.

"Oh, yes he did. I saw some of you helping him up on the dock."

"Oh, *that* kid," said Freddy. "He ain't in our club no more. He was such a loudmouth we voted him out for conduct unbecoming a scientist."

"He was givin' our club a bad name," said Dinky Poore.

"Okay, okay! Have it your own way. I just wanted to make sure I didn't miss anybody. Well! Lead on, gentlemen. You know the best eating places in town." And we all walked across the square to the Ye Olde Beef and Coffee Shoppe in the Bristol Hotel.

The Bristol Hotel used to be a pretty grand place in the days when salesmen and other people came to Mammoth Falls on the train and had to stay overnight to get the train out the next day. But nowadays it's kind of seedy and rundown, because hardly anybody stays overnight in Mammoth Falls anymore, and the Bristol and the other two little hotels in town have most of their rooms closed up—except when something fantastic happens, like the Air Force dropping a bomb, or something—and the same goes for the restaurants.

The Bristol used to have a magnificent dining room with tremendous crystal chandeliers, napkins, and white damask tablecloths and chairs with red velvet upholstery on them, and oriental rugs on the floor that were three inches deep, and beautiful ivory white paneling on the walls that was trimmed in gold leaf, and a ceiling that was painted a pale, greenish-blue with a lot of cherubs and angels flying around on it, and all that stuff.

My grandfather used to tell me about it, and there are still some pictures of it hanging on the wall behind the registration desk. My grandfather said when you had dinner there everybody was dressed up and you felt as if you were in some wonderful old palace with all the servants you wanted and you owned the place.

Now it's been converted into a meeting room that's used about twice a month for fund-raising dinners, or the Lions Club, or the PTA, or something like that. The walls have been covered with some kind of shiny wallboard, there are fluorescent lights in the ceiling in place of the chandeliers, there's some kind of linoleum on the floor, and there's a bare stage at one end of the room with two big horns for the public address system sticking out from the corners.

But old Mr. Pritchard, who runs the Bristol, says he couldn't make the dining room pay any more. He says you can't have nice things and progress, too. You just have to keep up with the times. The old Mammoth Falls Arms, that was even bigger and fancier than the Bristol, is a good example. It was a beautiful, big granite building with marble columns across the front and a big circular drive where people could drive their carriages in and hitch the horses to hitching posts. But almost nobody uses carriages anymore, and the

Mammoth Falls Arms was demolished by a wrecking crew before I was even born. There's a gasoline station on that corner now, and it's sort of a smelly eyesore in the town square. But, as Mr. Pritchard would say: "That's progress!" After all! What would you rather smell? Gasoline, or horse manure?

But, in spite of all the progress in Mammoth Falls in recent years, there are still a few good things left in town, and the Bristol's Ye Olde Beef and Coffee Shoppe is one of them. The hamburgers cost thirty-five cents, of course, whereas they're only fifteen cents at Jack The Flipper's right down the street. But they're a lot bigger, and you get an extra pickle and a piece of lettuce, besides. I never eat the lettuce, but it looks nice on the plate—which is a real piece of crockery instead of a hunk of cardboard like you get at Jack's. And you get a big paper napkin instead of a little skimpy one. I guess most everybody agrees the Bristol's hamburgers are the best you can get in town. But Jack The Flipper makes the best pancakes.

When we trooped in we saw Mr. MacComber sitting all alone in a booth, sipping a cup of coffee. Mr. Jenkins asked the waiter to pull a table up to the booth so we could all crowd in with him, and Dinky Poore, of course, ended up sitting out in the aisle where everybody bumped into his chair or hit him in the head with an elbow as they walked by.

"How do you want your hamburgers, boys?" the waiter asked, without even waiting to find out what we wanted.

"I don't want a hamburger," said Freddy Muldoon. "Just bring me a tuna fish and peanut butter sandwich and a lemon soda."

The waiter looked a little green, but he wrote down

the order and said: "I'll see. I don't know whether we
have that on the menu."

"And could I have some salt, please?" said Freddy.

The waiter reached over everybody's head and skidded
the saltcellar down the table toward him. And while
the rest of us were giving our orders, Freddy pulled a
big slice of watermelon out from under his shirt, salted
it liberally and started slurping it down as if he hadn't
had anything to eat all day.

"How about a napkin?" he said to the waiter, licking the
inside of his wrist where some of the juice had run down.

The waiter looked at him as if he were some sort of a
worm and handed him two napkins from the dispenser
on the table. Mr. MacComber sat there, quietly stirring
his coffee and shaking his head slowly from side to side
as he watched Freddy wolfing down the melon.

"You gotta see that kid to believe it," he said to Mr.
Jenkins, with a jerk of his head in Freddy's direction.
"Did I hear him say he wanted a tuna fish and peanut
butter sandwich?"

"I think that's what I heard," said Mr. Jenkins, "but I
was trying to forget it."

"Honest! If I sent the office a story on that kid, they
wouldn't believe it. They'd think I made it up."

"You'd probably get fired," Jenkins agreed. "You just
can't report everything you see, you know."

"Hey! I heard the colonel really shut off some of the
boys that wanted to go along and watch the diving
operation. That right?"

"Yeah, that's right. All they got was a good lecture on
how atom bombs are triggered."

"Well, they were kinda stupid," said Mr. MacComber.
"You gotta know when to stick your nose in, and when

not to. And there's no sense bustin' your nose against a brick wall. I imagine all they did was make themselves unpopular with the lieutenant."

"I don't imagine *you* did," Mr. Jenkins jibed at him.

"Well, I did. But look what I got. I got a story, and I've already phoned it in. All they got was a big fat "no" and a reputation for being stupid. That's what I mean! You gotta know when to stick your nose in."

"Okay!" Mr. Jenkins laughed. "All the same, I'd sure like to be there when they bring that bomb up. That's the story the whole country is waiting for."

"Ho, ho, ho and ho!" Mr. MacComber laughed. "You got about as much chance as a pig in a slaughterhouse. All you can do is cool your heels here with the rest of us until the Air Force says, 'Look, fellows! We got it. And if you behave yourselves, we'll let you take a picture of it from three hundred yards away.' So, relax and enjoy the ride. You're on an expense account, and you're over twenty-one, and your wife thinks you're out working hard...so, what have you got to worry about?"

"Would you really like to watch them raise the bomb?" Henry asked very quietly, as the waiter showed up with a three-foot tray full of hamburgers.

Mr. MacComber and Mr. Jenkins both looked at Henry.

"Oh, excuse me, 'Professor'," said Mr. MacComber, half-rising from his seat. "I almost forgot you were here."

"That's all right," said Henry. "I just wanted to mention that if you really want to watch them raise the bomb, you don't need Colonel March's permission."

"What do you mean, Henry?" said Mr. Jenkins, as he and Mr. MacComber exchanged glances. "Have you got some more magic up your sleeve?"

"There's no magic to it," said Henry, "All it takes is brains. That is, if you have the necessary equipment."

Mr. MacComber got caught with a mouthful of coffee and started choking, and he got all red in the face trying to stifle a laugh.

"I'm sorry. I didn't mean it that way," Henry said quickly. "What I mean is...well...Mr. Shorty has a telescopic lens with him, doesn't he?"

Mr. MacComber got caught again, and this time he spurted coffee all over his end of the table and Mr. Jenkins started pounding him on the back.

"*Mister* Shorty! Will you get a load of that!" he sputtered, when he was able to get a few words out of his mouth. "Professor Mulligan, you're a real card. Don't be so formal. The rest of us just call him *Doctor* Shorty!" And Mr. MacComber bellowed again and slapped the table and the tears were beginning to run down his cheeks, he was laughing so hard, and Henry was turning a little red.

"Yes, Shorty has a lot of lenses," said Mr. Jenkins. "It all depends on what you want to shoot."

"He'll need the biggest one he has," said Henry. "Do you have a tape deck and a monitor with you?"

"No. We use mostly film on these jobs, and they review it at the studio. What have you got in mind, Henry? If it's important, I can get WSEE to send the equipment down here. But it wouldn't get here until tonight, some time."

"We can do better than that," said Henry. "There's a TV station in Clinton—WEYE-TV—and I bet they'd lend you a tape deck and a monitor if you promised them a copy of the tape. You can drive over there and back in an hour."

"I know about WEYE," said Mr. Jenkins. "They feed my stuff back to WSEE for me. What would be on this tape that I promise to give them?"

"It would be the recovery operation," said Henry. "It's really very simple. There are lots of places in the hills west of Strawberry Lake where you can get a very good view of the area they'll be diving in. Like the old zinc mine, for instance. You could get up on the catwalk around that big crusher they used to break up the ore, and with a telescopic lens on the camera you could get in pretty close. Nobody would see you there, and it's too far up in the hills for any of the patrols to worry about."

A gleam started to come into Mr. Jenkins's eye. "Say, Henry! I think you've hit on something. Why didn't I think of that? But why do we need the video-recorder and the TV monitor?"

"Well," said Henry, starting to get a little red again as he pushed the piece of lettuce around on his plate, "I thought maybe, since I suggested the idea, you might let us all go along…and if we just plug Shorty's camera into the tape deck, and hook up the moni-tor…then we could all sit there and watch it…just like it was on TV!"

There was a soft splash, followed by a clatter of crockery, as Mr. MacComber's cigar fell into his coffee cup. He sat there looking at Henry with his jaw flopped open. Then he looked at Mr. Jenkins.

"Is this kid for real, Jake?" he said. "I don't know enough about your game to know whether he knows what he's talking about, but it sounds pretty good to me. Could this really be done?"

"Of course it could be done. It's done every day.

That's how they broadcast football games, and anything else that's done live. *Why* didn't I think of this myself? The only problem is whether we have enough battery power. This operation could last all afternoon."

"You shouldn't have to worry about batteries," said Henry. "Jeff's father has a three kilowatt-generator— you know, one of those Army surplus jobs mounted on a trailer. That's enough power for you, isn't it?"

"That's more than we need. Could we borrow it?"

"You'll have to borrow the jeep to tow it with, too," said Jeff. "But we'll need that anyway. You'd never get up to the zinc mine with that station wagon of yours."

"You guys are a regular gold mine," said Mr. MacComber. "Is there anything you don't have?"

"We're short on food," said Freddy Muldoon. "Yesterday I hardly ate anything, except some bananas."

Mr. MacComber choked on his coffee again. "I tell you what I'll do," he said. "If I can go along and watch this show, I'll bring the soda pop and hamburgers for lunch."

Everybody cheered and said "Okay!" and "We'll buy that!" and stuff like that, and Dinky Poore thumped Mr. MacComber on the back just as he was trying to get another mouthful of coffee. Mr. Jenkins shook his head in amusement and looked down the table at Freddy.

"Do you really mean you didn't have any lunch or supper yesterday? I can't believe it!"

"Oh, they don't count!" said Freddy. "It's what you get in between that keeps you filled up. My mother always says, if you want to be a scientist, you've got to eat well, so you have a strong body."

"I don't see why that's important for a scientist," said Mr. Jenkins.

"I don't, either," said Freddy. "But I agree with the eating part."

"You know what I think, Freddy? I think you made the whole thing up!" said Mr. Jenkins, as he got up from his seat and waved to the waiter for a check.

Two hours later we were all pushing on the jeep to help it get up the last steep incline to the crusher by the old zinc mine—all of us, that is, except Jeff who was driving, and Shorty the cameraman, who kept running around both sides of the jeep to make sure his camera gear and recording equipment weren't falling off. We parked the generator trailer at the base of the crusher and ran a power line up to the catwalk that ran on all four sides of it, about half-way up. Pretty soon we were all sitting up there watching the TV monitor while Mortimer and Dinky shinnied up two trees and cut back some branches that were blocking Shorty's view of the lake.

"Boy! This is just like having seats on the fifty-yard line at a Chinese funeral," said Mr. MacComber, as he propped himself up against the wall of the crusher. Then he tipped his hat down over his face, left an unlit cigar dangling from the side of his mouth, and closed his eyes. "Wake me up when the first act comes on, will you, Shorty?"

It was after two o'clock and the hamburgers were long gone before we saw any activity on the lake. Finally two patrol boats showed up, and a little later they were joined by a small tug, towing what looked like a big raft with a derrick on it. We'd never seen anything like them on the lake before, but Mr. Jenkins explained that they were Army engineer equipment that had been brought in on railroad flat cars the day after the bomb was lost.

We sat and watched for hours while divers kept going over the side of one of the patrol boats and coming back up to have their air tanks refilled. Shorty had a good zoom lens on his camera, and whenever something seemed to be happening on one of the boats he would zoom in and give us a close-up of the action. It was pretty exciting. You could almost read the lips of some of the characters on the decks of the patrol boats. But it was also pretty dull. Nothing seemed to be happening that could give us an indication of when they would start raising the bomb. Colonel March was on board the boat the divers were using, and they kept coming back up and reporting to him with a lot of gestures that we couldn't figure out. But it was apparent that they had run into some kind of a problem.

"They sure should have found that bomb by now," Mortimer Dalrymple muttered. "Maybe we should have drawn them a map."

"Maybe the bomb just 'sploded and disappeared," said Dinky Poore.

"Nuts!" said Freddy Muldoon. "If it had 'sploded, we'd of heard it."

"Under all that water?" Dinky challenged him.

"Yeah! Ain't you never seen one a' them mushrooms from an atom bomb? It's bigger'n a house, and goes way up in the sky!"

"Sure, I seen 'em. Lots of 'em. But maybe this mushroom went down instead of up."

Freddy Muldoon's lips curled in contempt, and he sort of snorted. "Boy, you don't know nothin' about science, do you?"

"I know a mushroom when I see one, and we ain't seen one!"

"All of which means the bomb never 'sploded," said Freddy, with exaggerated patience. "If it had, you'd be dead! Maybe that would of been a good idea," he added, as an afterthought. Then Freddy burped, as he often does.

"Oh, boy, you big gas bag!" Dinky spat at him, clenching his fists. Then he ran at Freddy with his arms flailing, and Freddy took off down the catwalk and disappeared 'round the corner with Dinky in hot pursuit.

By this time Mr. MacComber had practically collapsed on the catwalk from laughter, and the cigar he had been smoking rolled off the edge and dropped into a pile of dead leaves. Jeff went down the ladder to retrieve it before it could start a fire, and Mortimer dashed to the opposite corner of the crusher and caught Freddy and Dinky in full stride as they charged around it. He made them shake hands by threatening to knock their heads together if they didn't and they both quieted down. My old man says if you want to stop people from fighting, all you have to do is threaten them with something worse. I don't know whether it's true, but it sure worked in this case. Freddy and Dinky just sat down in front of the TV with their backs against the crusher wall and glared at each other.

We watched while the divers made another descent, and when they came back up they had a long conference with Colonel March and an Army officer who was on board with two men in civilian clothes. While they were talking, one of the patrol boats left. It came back later, towing a big red buoy in its wake. The divers went over the side again and anchored the buoy right where our balloon was tethered. Then they hauled in our balloon, deflated it, and all three of the boats headed back for shore, with the big raft trailing behind them.

"I wonder what that's all about," Mr. MacComber grunted, as he hoisted himself back onto his feet. "Seems to me they didn't do anything but have one gab fest after another."

"Beats me!" said Mr. Jenkins. "Maybe we'd better get back into town and see if they have some kind of a statement for us. It's already four o'clock and I've got to drive to Clinton to feed this stuff back to the station."

"I'm sorry they didn't bring the bomb up," said Henry. "I can't figure out what went wrong."

"That's all right!" said Mr. Jenkins, patting Henry on the back. "You put on a pretty good show. Nobody else has pictures of this operation, and I oughta make a pretty big splash with it."

"You'll make a splash, all right!" Mr. MacComber observed. "And some of it might get in your eye. Wait'll those Air Force boys tune in the news tonight. They'll never figure out *how* you got those pictures, but they'll probably make sure you don't get any more."

"That's one of the risks you take for a scoop," Mr. Jenkins shrugged. "If they get nosy, I'll just refer them to Professor Mulligan. He figured it all out."

We all felt a little disappointed that we hadn't seen the bomb brought to the surface, but at the same time we were burning with curiosity about the reason for all the lengthy conferences on board the patrol boat. So we loaded everything into the jeep as fast as we could and bounced back down the trail to where we had left Mr. Jenkins's station wagon. When we got back into town we went straight to the Bristol Hotel, which was the headquarters for most of the reporters who had flocked into town. A lot of them were lounging around in the lobby, playing gin rummy, or poker, or watching TV, or just snoring in the lounge chairs.

"Where you guys been?" one of them asked. "You missed all the excitement."

"Uh...we just went out in the country for a picnic," Mr. Jenkins answered. "What's the excitement? What happened?"

"Farrell, over there, just drew a pat royal flush and broke up the poker game, that's all! You shoulda been here. You coulda lost some money."

"Oh is that all? I thought maybe something important happened."

"You'd think it was important if you'd been sitting there with a full house, like I was. He couldn't have picked a better time to do it. Hennessey drew to a straight flush and hit it, and we went to the limit. Musta been three hundred bucks in that pot!"

"I told you it was only about two-and-a-quarter," said the man named Farrell, without even opening his eyes. "And *I* put about half of it in there, meetin' your stupid raises. You must have learned your poker at a charity bazaar, or somethin'."

"That's life for you," said Mr. MacComber, with a sly wink. "The winners tell jokes, and the losers tell lies."

"Did you take all those kids on the picnic?" one of the gin rummy players asked.

"No, they took *us*!" Mr. MacComber answered, with a loud guffaw. "It cost me eight bucks for soda pop and hamburgers. What do you hear from the Air Force? Anything?"

"Nothing!" said the gin rummy player, looking at his watch. "We gotta call that lieutenant pretty soon, though. It's almost deadline time for my paper."

"Wonder if they found that bomb yet," said one of the other players.

"Yeah! I wonder!" said Mr. MacComber, as he wedged himself into a telephone booth next to the one Mr. Jenkins was using.

Both he and Mr. Jenkins were a long time on the telephone; and before they finished, the other reporters were knocking on the doors, trying to get them out so they could place their own calls. When Mr. Jenkins finally came out, he held his hands up to quiet the crowd in front of the booth.

"It's no use, boys," he said. "I finally got to talk to Colonel March, himself, and he absolutely refuses to make any statement at this time."

"Well, did they find the bomb?" a dozen reporters asked at once.

"If they did, they won't admit it."

"But what about that big orange balloon those kids staked out on the lake? Did they send divers down there?"

"Yes, they did," said Mr. Jenkins.

"And they claim they didn't find anything?"

"The whole thing was just a hoax, then?"

"You mean we suckered for some kind of a magic show that kid put on?"

"Hold on a minute! Hold on!" said Mr. Jenkins, putting his hands up again. "They didn't say they *hadn't* found the bomb."

"Well, you just said they did."

"No I didn't...I said they wouldn't make any statement.

They wouldn't say they had found the bomb, and they wouldn't say they hadn't. They just said, 'No comment!' Personally, I think they *did* find it."

"Why? How come you know so much?"

"Because they took down the balloon and towed a red buoy out there to mark the spot. They wouldn't anchor a buoy there unless they were intending to go back there again."

"That makes sense. But how come you know all this?"

"I just know it, that's all," said Mr. Jenkins. "You'll just have to take my word for it."

"And a pig's neck I will!" said the sloppy looking reporter that always had his coat over his arm and his necktie undone. "How do we know you're not trying to put us off the scent, Jenkins? How do we know you ain't already filed the story and got a big jump on us? Hey! Holy Moses! I bet that's why you took so long in that phone booth. You weren't talkin' to no colonel! You were talkin' to your home office, puttin' your story on tape!"

"Now, wait a minute, wait a minute!" Mr. Jenkins pleaded. But he might as well have whistled into the wind. The other reporters were climbing all over him in a rush to get into the phone booth.

"You got a nerve, Jenkins!"

"I'm gonna call the colonel, myself."

"Nuts to that! I'm gonna call the Pentagon!"

"What a bunch of patsies we've been!"

"Thanks a lot, Jenkins! Remind me to do *you* a favor sometime."

Then the group sort of exploded in all directions—up the stairs, down the stairs, out in the street—searching for telephones. Mr. MacComber came out of the next phone booth and stood there quietly.

"What's all the excitement?" he asked, casually.

"Nothing," said Mr. Jenkins. "The boys think we're pulling the wool over their eyes. They think I know something they don't know, and I won't let them in on the story."

"You *do* know something that they don't know."

"What's that?"

"You know how old your mother is!" said Mr. MacComber, and he stalked off toward the registration desk.

But before he got there he felt Henry Mulligan's fingers grabbing his sleeve. Henry was gesturing frantically toward the other side of the lobby. A tall, rangy man with a heavy black moustache was just disappearing through the doorway marked "Bar & Grill." Mr. MacComber turned around just in time to see the man. Then he looked at Henry, and Henry looked at him.

"What do you think?" said Mr. MacComber.

"I think it's one of the divers we saw on the deck of the patrol boat," said Henry, "but I can't be sure."

"I can't either," said Mr. MacComber, "because Shorty didn't always have his camera in good focus on those close-ups."

"But I noticed a red line across his forehead," said Henry. "That could mean he'd been wearing a tight helmet."

"You're a smart kid," said Mr. MacComber. "I think it's time I bought somebody a drink." And with a wink to Henry, he strode across the lobby and was swallowed up by the crowd in the Bar & Grill.

That night, the town of Mammoth Falls slept on tenterhooks—that is, if anybody slept at all. By late evening, the Air Force had still refused to make any statement at all about the bomb, and all sorts of rumors were flying about the town again. I guess some people figured the Air Force just hadn't found the bomb and didn't want to admit it. And a lot more figured our balloon stunt was just a big hoax and we'd led the Air Force on a wild goose chase and they were too embarrassed to talk. But most people would rather believe something spectacular, if they have a choice, and the people of Mammoth Falls are no exception. So there was a lot of talk on the street corners and over back fences about a rumor that the bomb was about to explode and the Air Force couldn't do anything to stop it. The people that believed this one were packing a little bedding and food into their cars and taking off for anywhere they thought was far enough away from the danger zone. There were streams of cars and pickup trucks clogging the roads leading out of town, east, west, north, and south. And every gasoline station in town had pumped its tanks dry by early evening.

But the oddest rumor floating around town was a report that the Air Force had discovered it hadn't lost a bomb, after all, and that what had fallen in the lake was just a wing tank full of jet fuel. A lot of people believed this one, because they wanted to believe it, and they figured the Air Force was just stalling for time while it figured out how to explain the fact it had kept the whole town on its ear for four days with a phony bomb scare.

I guess most everybody left in town had his nose glued to the tube when the late TV news came on at 11:00 o'clock that night, hoping the Air Force would clear up the mystery, one way or the other. The Air Force didn't. But Mr. MacComber must have bought more than one drink for that big man with the black moustache that Henry figured was one of the divers, 'cause he blabbed pretty good.

I was sitting in the middle of our living room floor in my skivvies, with the volume on the TV turned down low so my mother wouldn't hear it, and all the lights out, trying to munch potato chips without making any noise. About the first five minutes of the news was all about the lost bomb, of course, and I sat there cheering under my breath and slapping the floor while they showed Mr. Jenkins interviewing Jeff and Henry on the end of the dock, and Colonel March's car buried under Jaspar Okeby's watermelons, and about thirty-seven seconds of the four hours of tape Shorty shot on the diving operations. Then there was a lot of gobbledy-gook about why the Air Force wouldn't talk, and how come they hadn't found the bomb yet, and what the latest congressman who wanted some publicity had to say about the situation, and junk like that. I was just about to turn the thing off and get up to bed, when the words SPECIAL BULLETIN flashed on the screen, and an announcer said:

"LADIES AND GENTLEMEN, WE INTERRUPT OUR REGULARLY SCHEDULED NEWS BROADCAST TO BRING YOU THIS SPECIAL BULLETIN FROM THE WIRES OF THE ASSOCIATED PRESS: MAMMOTH FALLS—THE ASSOCIATED PRESS REPORTED TONIGHT IT HAD LEARNED FROM AN UNUSUALLY RELIABLE SOURCE THAT THE NUCLEAR DEVICE REPORTED MISSING BY THE AIR FORCE FOUR DAYS AGO HAS DEFINITELY BEEN LOCATED BY AIR FORCE DIVERS WORKING IN AN AREA OF STRAWBERRY LAKE THAT

HAD PREVIOUSLY BEEN SEARCHED WITHOUT SUCCESS. THE MISSING BOMB IS REPORTED TO BE LODGED IN A SMALL CAVE, OR CREVICE, IN A SUBMERGED RIDGE ABOUT THREE HUNDRED YARDS OFFSHORE, AND PRECISELY WHERE A GROUP OF LOCAL YOUNGSTERS HAD PREDICTED IT WOULD BE FOUND."

"Whoopee-ee-ee!" I yelled at the top of my lungs. And then I clapped my hand over my mouth. Sure enough, my mother's sleepy voice came from upstairs.

"Is that you, Charlie? What on earth are you doing?"

I didn't answer. I had my ear pressed against the TV so I wouldn't miss anything.

"THE INFORMANT, WHO IS NOT IDENTIFIED IN THE DISPATCH, TOLD THE ASSOCIATED PRESS THAT REMOVAL OF THE BOMB POSED A SEVERE SAFETY PROBLEM FOR THE AIR FORCE AND THE U.S. ARMY ENGINEERS ASSIGNED TO THE SEARCH AND RECOVERY OPERATION. OFFICIALS ARE FEARFUL THAT ANY ATTEMPT TO REMOVE THE WEAPON FROM THE NARROW CREVICE COULD RESULT IN A RUPTURING OF THE BOMB CASING AND THE POSSIBLE RELEASE OF FISSIONABLE MATERIALS INTO THE WATERS OF THE LAKE. ACCORDING TO THE SOURCE, AIR FORCE OFFICIALS ARE FACED WITH THE DILEMMA OF RISKING CONTAMINATION OF THE LAKE AND THE IMMEDIATE SURROUNDING AREA BY ATTEMPTING TO RECOVER THE BOMB, OR LEAVING THE TOWN OF MAMMOTH FALLS WITH A TWENTY-MEGATON 'TIME BOMB' FOREVER SITTING ON ITS DOORSTEP."

"SO FAR, AIR FORCE OFFICIALS HAVE BEEN RELUCTANT TO MAKE ANY STATEMENT ABOUT TODAY'S SEARCH OPERATIONS. SPOKESMEN AT NEARBY WESTPORT FIELD TONIGHT REFUSED TO CONFIRM OR DENY REPORTS THAT THE MISSING BOMB HAD BEEN FOUND. A TERSE 'NO COMMENT' WAS THEIR ONLY RESPONSE TO QUERIES ABOUT THE ASSOCIATED PRESS STORY."

"WE REPEAT—THE ASSOCIATED PRESS IN A LATE BULLETIN TONIGHT REPORTS THAT AIR FORCE DIVERS HAVE FOUND THE NUCLEAR BOMB ACCIDENTALLY DROPPED FROM A SAC BOMBER FOUR DAYS AGO IN THE VICINITY OF MAMMOTH FALLS. AIR FORCE OFFICIALS HAVE REFUSED TO CONFIRM OR DENY THE REPORT."

"WE NOW RETURN YOU TO YOUR LOCAL PRO-GRAMMING."

I switched the set off and started tiptoeing out of the room. Then I tiptoed back and stood in the middle of the living room wondering whether I should call Jeff or Henry. Maybe they hadn't heard the news. I started toward the telephone, but stopped. Maybe they'd be in bed, I thought. Just then my mother called again.

"Charlie!...Charlie!...Why don't you answer me? What are you doing down there?"

"I was just letting the cat in," I lied. "Come on, kitty, kitty, kitty," I called, letting the front screen door slam a couple of times.

"That's funny! The cat's right up here with me."

"I guess that's why he wouldn't come in," I said, slam-ming the front door shut. Some days nothing goes right, I thought to myself, as I tromped up the stairs.

I was dead tired, but for some reason, after I flicked the light out I could no more get to sleep than I could shovel steam with a steam shovel. I kept thinking about what that news announcer had said: "...a twenty megaton 'time bomb' forever sitting on its doorstep!" Just like the sword of Damocles, I kept saying to myself. And I started worrying about how that old Greek character felt, sitting under that sword while he was trying to enjoy his supper. And I guess I just plain worried myself to sleep, because all I remember is that I had one of those horrible nightmares where I was sitting among hundreds of people in a big banquet hall in nothing but my underwear, trying to cover myself with the tablecloth and still keep out from under a big sword that was swinging back and forth above my head.

I don't know why it is, but we run around half the summer with nothing covering our hides but a scanty pair of shorts and think nothing of it, yet we have a dream about being caught out in public in our underwear and there's something downright embarrassing about it. And this dream was no exception. I can remember grabbing a banana off the table and trying to stick the peels on the front of my undershirt so they'd look like a gold "M" and people would think I was on the Mammoth Falls track team, but it didn't work. The peels just kept falling off. Then Mayor Scragg climbed up on the table right in front of me, and he was not only fully-clothed, but was wearing a big, heavy overcoat to boot and was brandishing his umbrella in one hand. He kept swinging the umbrella at the sword as it came by, and I kept ducking my head every time he swung, hoping he wouldn't split any hairs. Finally, he tossed the umbrella aside, grabbed a huge watermelon off the table, and held it in the path of the swinging sword, which cut off a big slice each time it passed by. I kept dodging right and left to keep the slices from plopping onto my bare shoulders, and every time I did I'd lose my grip on the tablecloth and everybody at the banquet table would turn and point at me and laugh uproariously. But nobody tried to stop Mayor Scragg, who was cackling with fiendish glee every time the sword cut off another slice.

Then four lackeys came trudging into the hall with the whole carcass of a roast ox suspended between two truncheons and they brought it right up to the head table and plopped it right in front of me. And there inside the carcass sat Freddy Muldoon, tearing big chunks of roast beef off with his fingernails and stuffing them into his mouth. Every time I'd open my mouth to plead with Freddy to do something about the sword, no sound would come out, and Freddy would just sit there and rub his stomach and burp in my face. I got so mad at him I got to tearing at the tablecloth, trying to pull Freddy and the ox carcass closer to me, or get out from under the sword, and the tablecloth kept tearing into shreds, and then something sharp stabbed me right in the back and I must have jumped twenty feet straight up the air.

Somehow I landed on my feet, and suddenly everything was light, and there was my mother standing in front of me with the kitchen broom in her hands.

"What time is it?" I asked, rubbing my eyes.

"It's time you were up, sleepyhead!"

I could have kicked myself for asking the question, but I guess I'll never learn.

The Bubble Bursts

When the TV news broadcast about the damaged bomb hit Washington, it must have lifted the dome right off the Capitol a few feet, because all kinds of politicians and other creatures started scampering out of the place and heading for Mammoth Falls. You'd have thought radiation was good for people, the way high-ranking moguls came pouring into town next morning.

While I was eating breakfast it seemed as though a plane buzzed our house every three minutes in the approach lane to Westport Field. "What's going on?" I finally asked my mother, after four or five planes had rattled the windows.

"If you'd get up in time, sleepyhead, you could hear the seven o'clock news. Then you wouldn't have to ask people." And she plopped another bowl of cereal down in front of me.

"C'mon, Ma! What is it? What'd they say?"

"Eat your cereal first."

Holy Mackerel, that makes me mad when people do things like that.

"Gosh, Ma…I already ate a whole bowl. Pretty soon I'm gonna have oats growin' out of my ears."

"So what? Who could see them?" she laughed. "When are you going down to Mr. Carver's to get your hair cut?"

"As soon as I find out what's going on," I said, with sudden inspiration, and she laughed again.

"Okay, goose. Then I'll tell you."

My mother and I usually have a good time together, but she can be a pest sometimes.

"They said on the radio that all kinds of people from Washington were coming here to investigate about the bomb. I guess they think they found it, but there was something about they were afraid it had a *rupture*, or something, and that could be dangerous. I remember your father had a rupture once, when he was a young man, and Doctor Danberry said there wasn't anything dangerous about it at all, but I guess it's different with a bomb, and…."

"C'mon, Ma! I heard all that already. What about all these people coming from Washington. Anybody important? Like the President, maybe?"

"You heard all that already? Oh, that's what you were doing up late last night. You sneaked downstairs and turned the TV on, didn't you?"

"No, I didn't. I sneaked downstairs and turned it *off*," I said, trying to keep from choking on my oatmeal.

"Char…l…i…e!"

"Yes, I did. Scout's honor!"

"Well, who left it on?"

"I did, but that was earlier."

"When was that?"

"The first time I sneaked downstairs."

A hot pot holder hit me in the back of the neck and I spilled some oatmeal and cream all down the front of my T-shirt; and when I coughed, some of the oatmeal went up my nose, and I figured this was just gonna be one of those days. Boy! Did I have a premonition!

"Well, what big shots are coming in here from Washington?" I asked, when I could get the words out.

"Practically everybody. The man on the radio said people from the Atomic Energy Commission, the Secretary of the Air Force, the Secretary of Defense, the Postmaster General, and I don't know who else."

"The Postmaster General? What's he gonna do? Sell stamps?"

"They didn't say," my mother laughed again. "But I heard the other day he was thinking of running for president next year, and I guess he thinks the trip will do him good."

Friday morning is a crazy time to get your hair cut, but I figured I might as well—not only because I'd promised my mother I would, but also because I might have a chance to pump some of the old geezers that hang around Ned Carver's shop and maybe find out more about what was happening. Talk about great minds with but a single thought! Dinky Poore and Homer Snodgrass were already sitting in line, waiting to get their hair cut, when I got there. I plopped into the seat next to Homer, who was picking his nose, and stared at Dinky, who was gazing at the far wall as if he was in a trance. He looked pale as a ghost.

"What's the matter, Dinky? Are you sick?" I asked.

"Nope!"

"How come you're so pale, then?"

"My mother made me take a bath after I got home last night."

"Oh!"

"I told her she'd rub all the tan off if she scrubbed that hard—but she went ahead and did it anyway." Dinky gulped hard, once, and a tear started to trickle out of his left eye.

"That's too bad," I said.

"Yeah!" said Dinky, gulping again and fighting hard to hold back the tears. "A fella works hard all summer to build up a good tan, and some creepy gal has to foul the whole thing up."

"That's mothers for you," I said, digging Homer in the ribs with my elbow.

"Yeah, I hope the President sends a woman to the moon pretty soon. Then maybe there'll be one less on earth," said Dinky, getting his handkerchief out to blow his nose.

Old Ned Perkins was sitting in the front barber chair and Mr. Carver was fussing around his half-bald head as if it was some kind of a work of art. I don't know why it is, but every time I go to the barber, I sit there and watch him work over some old geezer for thirty-five or forty minutes, just snipping away endlessly with the tips of his scissors at hairs you can't even see on a head with so little on it you wonder why the old coot thought he needed a haircut in the first place. When it finally comes to my turn, he clips all the hair off my head in less than ten minutes, snaps the hair cloth out in front of the chair, and holds his hand out for the money.

Come to think of it, I guess I do know why it is.

Mr. Carver sizes up his customers pretty shrewdly, and if he thinks some old character has thirty-five minutes of good information in him, he wants to give him plenty of time to get it all out. When a kid gets in the chair, he figures he isn't going to hear anything he hasn't heard before, and it gives him a chance to show everybody how fast he can cut a head of hair when he really wants to. All the same, I hope they pass a law someday giving kids equal time in barber chairs.

We just sat there for a while, twiddling our thumbs and leafing through the old magazines and the dog-eared copy of *The Farmer's Almanac* Mr. Carver always has in his shop, with our ears wide open. Ned Perkins was giving his opinions about the atom bomb to Mr. Carver, but loud enough so he could be sure everyone in the shop could get the full benefit of what he had to say.

"I figger them contraptions is dangerous enough, all right," he was saying, "but I also figger the Air Force knows what it's doin'. My son was in the Air Force when it was jest called the Army Air Corps," he added, moving his head away from Mr. Carver's scissors long enough to look around the room, "and he knows that outfit from top to bottom. And he says they know what they're doin'!"

Just then, Charlie Brown, the town treasurer, came in and placed his straw hat carefully on one of the hooks. Everybody said "good morning" to him, but nobody kidded him about his new shoes—which they usually do, just because he's also the only undertaker in town and is always wearing shoes that look brand new, except they're always black. This particular morning everyone was more interested in what Charlie might have to say about all the people coming in from

Washington; because, as a member of the Town
Council he was supposed to know everything that was
going on.

Charlie didn't disappoint them. He didn't even sit
down though, when one of the other customers moved
over one seat so Charlie could have his favorite chair.
He started spouting out just about everything he knew
about the situation, while he strode up and down the
room, either wiping his glasses or re-lighting his cigar
at every turn.

"I feel kind of sorry for Colonel March," he said. "You
fellas don't know him like I do, but he's a real gentleman. Now he's got all these big-wigs from Washington
breathing down his neck, and about all they want to do
is hold a press conference and get out of town as fast as
they can...and leave him with the problem."

Charlie took two good puffs on his cigar and coughed
three times.

"Now, as I see it, we've got a very touchy situation
here in Mammoth Falls. Maybe this'll put us on the
map...if it don't blow us off of it. But I guess we're the
only town in the whole country—maybe the whole
world—that ever had an atom bomb sitting right
beside it that nobody can get to."

"We got to it, Mr. Brown," said Dinky, raising his
hand.

"Shut up, sonny," said Charlie Brown. "Like I was
saying, everybody keeps criticizing Colonel March. But
he's doin' the best he can, and he's a fine man. Now
he's got all these rinky-dinks from Washington flyin' in
here, and what they know about handling atom bombs
you could probably stick up your nose and it wouldn't
even make you sneeze."

"You can say that again!" said Ned Perkins from the chair.

"Okay! I'll say it again," said Charlie Brown, not even pausing for breath. "What they know about handling atom bombs you could probably stick up your nose and it wouldn't even make you sneeze."

Old Elmer Crabtree, sitting in the rocker in the corner, cackled loudly at that one. Elmer doesn't have a hair on his head, and why he hangs around the barber shop so much is a mystery to me. But I guess he's a pretty good listener, so Mr. Carver likes to have him on hand. "Go get 'em, Charlie!" he said.

"Yeah! You give it to 'em, Charlie!"

"Let's hear it, Charlie!"

Everybody in town likes to see Charlie Brown get his dander up. He won the state oratory prize when he was in Mammoth Falls High School, and he was captain of the debating team at Slippery Rock College for three years. He can sure lay the language out when he gets wound up, and it makes people whistle, and cheer, and stamp their feet. Right now he was wound up good and the words were just tumbling out of his mouth as though he didn't even have to think about what he was saying. The faster he talked, the faster he paced up and down; and the cigar in his mouth was getting chewed to ragged brown shreds.

"Now, I didn't sleep too much last night, and I guess nobody else did. It's not a very comfortable thought that you might get blown to smithereens before you can even get the bedclothes off. But then I fell to thinkin' about how Colonel March felt. And all those other fellows out there at the air base. How much sleep did they get? If we're gonna get blown to kingdom come, they're gonna get blown right along with us. And besides that, they've had everybody in the country yackin' at them about how come they couldn't find that bomb. I'm tellin' you, I woke up feeling sorry for the whole bunch of them."

"How come you woke up if you didn't get no sleep, Charlie?" said Elmer Crabtree.

"Shut up, Elmer!" said Charlie Brown. "On second thought, that's not such a bad question. Remind me to buy you a haircut some time."

The laughter that greeted that one practically rattled the mirrors on Ned Carver's walls, and Elmer's bald head turned red all over. The pipe dropped from his mouth and clattered on the floor as he opened his mouth again.

"I heard tell they might just have to leave that bomb right where it is...forever, maybe."

"I heard the same thing on the radio this morning," said Charlie. "But I know those politicians in Washington won't let 'em do it. You know what I heard out at the air base this morning when we went out there to meet those people comin' in?"

Everybody said "What?" even though they knew Charlie was going to tell them anyway, because they know Charlie likes to be teased a little bit before he gives out important information. Besides, it gives him a few seconds to wipe his glasses and settle them back in the notch above his nose. But they always slip down again, right away. I bet I've seen Charlie Brown wipe his glasses eight or ten times in five minutes.

"What was it Charlie?"

"What'd you hear?"

"Well I heard one of those bigwigs tellin' the press...

I think he was from that there Atom Commission, or whatever they call it...he was tellin' them he'd give the Air Force just two days to get that bomb out of that hole, and if they couldn't do it the Commission would take over and get somebody in here who could."

"Hey, that's good!"

"No, it ain't good," said Charlie Brown. "Like I said, Colonel March is a fine man, and he's got his career in the Air Force to think about. He's been a good commander out there, and I'd hate to see him go. And...."

"See him go?"

"Is he leavin'?"

"Is he gettin' outa town like them other nuts and leavin' us here with that infernal contraption in the lake? He's got a nerve!" said Jaspar Okeby, who had just come in the door.

"Jaspar, you're a nut!" said Charlie Brown, spitting the words out of the side of his mouth the cigar wasn't on. "When you come in to get fitted for a coffin, remind me to get your head stuffed. We might want to hang it on the wall somewheres in the Town Hall. I didn't say he was leaving...leastways not right now. But you boys don't realize the spot he's in. The townsfolk are bangin' him on the head, the newspapers are bangin' him on the head, and now half the big shots in Washington are bangin' him on the head. He's been banged on the head so much I'll bet it hurts to get a haircut!"

Charlie waited for the laughter to die down, then went on.

"You ever been in a spot where no matter which way you turn you can't see a friend? That's the kind of spot Colonel March is in right now. Not bein' able to find that bomb, and then havin' them smart-aleck kids show everybody where it was, didn't make him look too good, you know. So I expect when this is all over the Air Force'll find some other job for him. That is, unless he can figure some way to get that bomb outa there without any trouble. And if this atom fella means what he said, the colonel hasn't got much time."

All of a sudden I started feeling sorry for Colonel March, myself. I figured I'd better get out of there, and go find Henry and Jeff and tell them what was going on.

"I'm gonna beat it," I said to Homer. "I can't waste the whole morning here."

But Homer grabbed my elbow and pointed out to the street. Mr. Jenkins and Shorty, the cameraman, were heading for the barber shop, lugging their equipment with them.

"Good morning, gentlemen," said Mr. Jenkins, with his most professional smile, as he held the door open for Shorty to squeeze in with all his gear. Then he introduced himself to Mr. Carver.

"We'd just like to get a little local color, if you don't mind." And Mr. Jenkins smiled at everyone in the shop.

"Ain't much color 'round here this time of year," said Elmer Crabtree. "You'd best come back in the fall. 'Long about mid-October them hills west of Strawberry Lake is jest gorgeous."

Mr. Jenkins gave him a polite nod. "I hope we can come back," he said. "Right now, we'd like to get a few opinions on how you people feel about the lake being drained."

"*Lake* being drained?"

"What lake?"

"What you talkin' about, mister?"

Everybody in the shop had risen from his seat. Mr. Carver dropped his scissors on the floor, and Charlie Brown's glasses had dropped right to the end of his nose. Mr. Jenkins hastened to explain.

"You mean you haven't heard about it yet? No...I guess you couldn't have heard yet. But the story's gone out on the wires already. Commissioner Johnson from the AEC said he'd ask the Department of Interior to take charge if the Air Force doesn't have the bomb out of there within two days. And the Secretary of the Interior in Washington said he'd order the Army Engineers to drain the lake so they can get into that cave and get the bomb out safely."

"You mean drain the whole lake?"

"Would you mind repeating that?" said Mr. Jenkins, sticking his skinny microphone right up to Charlie Brown's nose.

"Get that thing outa here!" said Charlie, brushing the microphone aside. "I don't talk through my nose, you know."

"I'm sorry! I just wanted to get your reaction to the report that the lake might be drained."

"I'll show you my reaction," Charlie Brown snorted. *"There ain't gonna be no lake drained.* Leastways, not while I'm alive and able to kick!" And with that, Charlie Brown slapped his hat back onto his head so hard he bit right through his cigar, and the biggest part of it dribbled down the front of his shirt and rolled onto the floor as he stomped out of the barber shop.

To say that pandemonium broke loose in Mammoth Falls as the news of the lake draining spread around town, is to put it mildly. Outraged citizens were besieging the

Town Hall, and protest meetings were being held all over the place. Abigail Larrabee got busy and began organizing her women to march on the air base. We heard that a group of them were petitioning Congressman Hawkins to walk barefoot with them all the way to Washington; but his office said he had suddenly been called back to Washington, and he couldn't be reached. Like most everyone else in town, the Mad Scientists' Club had an emergency meeting as soon as Jeff could call us all together.

"Phew!" said Freddy Muldoon, fanning his nose with his skullcap. "Imagine all them dead fish!"

" 'Specially Old Pincushion!" I said. "We never would get a chance to catch him."

"Okay! Everybody quiet down!" said Jeff, rapping for order. "I called this meeting because Henry had another brainstorm. Give out with it, Henry."

Henry leaned forward and the front legs of his piano stool hit the floor. "Well, I think I've figured out a way to get that bomb out of there without draining the lake," he began. "Now, Colonel March has only got two days to...."

Just then there was a knock at the door. Freddy opened it, because we had appointed him Sergeant-at-Arms, and there stood Mr. Jenkins and Mr. MacComber.

"May we come in?" Mr. Jenkins asked.

"No!" said Freddy.

"Well isn't this the Mad Scientists' Club?" he asked, shading his eyes from the light so he could peer inside. Freddy closed the door half way.

"Do you know the password?"

"I'm afraid I don't."

"Then you can't come in," said Freddy. "And tell those photographers to get out of here, too. This is a security area."

"Knock it off, Freddy! Knock it off!" Jeff called out. "Come on in, Mr. Jenkins. You're welcome, anytime."

"Except when we're in executive session," Mortimer added.

Mr. Jenkins and Mr. MacComber squeezed inside, followed by a couple of other reporters and three photographers, but they had to come in single-file because Freddy kept the door half-closed.

"We just wanted to thank you for breaking the story for us," Mr. Jenkins said, "and a couple of the boys that didn't believe you, wanted to apologize."

"We didn't break the story," said Henry, modestly. "That diver Mr. MacComber cornered in the bar is the one who really did it."

"Yeah, he sure did!" said Mr. MacComber, with a rumble of laughter. "That guy spends too much time in the water. He couldn't stand anything stronger!" And he laughed so hard he inhaled a lot of cigar smoke, and ended up in a coughing fit.

"Also, the wire services are asking for pictures of you," said Mr. Jenkins. "Could we take them right here in your clubhouse?"

"If I'd known that, I'd have taken a bath," said Homer Snodgrass.

"I don't think the dirt'll show in this light," said one of the photographers, as he began snapping shots at random.

"What do you think about them draining the lake?" Mr. Jenkins asked after the picture taking had finished.

"It's stupid!" said Freddy Muldoon.

"It's not really necessary," said Henry. "I know a way they could get that bomb out of there without going to all that trouble."

"I see the Professor's been thinking again," said Mr. MacComber, nudging Mr. Jenkins with his elbow. "I know what you're gonna do, Professor. You're gonna part the waters and drive a truck right out to that cave, and haul that bomb in, aren't you? Could we watch this time, if I promise to buy the hamburgers again?"

You could see Henry starting to burn red behind the ears. Henry doesn't take kidding too well, but he did manage a little laugh. "No! That's too much like work. But that cave is a sealed cavity. All you have to do is pump air into it until you have enough pressure to force the water out of the cave. Then divers could go in there and build a crate around that bomb to protect it. Then, all you have to do is inflate a couple of life rafts around it, and when you let the water back in the cave, you can float the bomb right out."

Mr. MacComber's eyes had bugged out. But Mr. Jenkins looked very serious. "Is the mouth of the cave big enough for that?"

"Sure it is," I said.

And Mortimer agreed. "You might bump the sides a little, but if the bomb is protected, that wouldn't matter. It'd be a lot easier than tryin' to winch it out of there with a cable."

Mr. Jenkins and Mr. MacComber looked at each other. "Maybe we got another story," said Mr. MacComber. "Are you sure this would work, Henry…er…Professor?"

Henry thought for a minute. Then he said: "It would be very interesting to find out. Because, if it doesn't work, they'll have to rewrite all the textbooks on basic physics."

"I see what you mean," Mr. MacComber grunted. "Please excuse me for asking such a stupid question, Professor." Then he and Mr. Jenkins made their way out the door, followed by the other reporters and photographers. But Mr. MacComber stuck his head back in and winked at Henry. "If I were you, I'd let Colonel March know about your idea. Right now, he needs all the help he can get...believe me!"

"That's just fine!" said Jeff, after they all had left. "But just how do we get to Colonel March?"

"We could write him a letter," said Dinky Poore.

"Great idea!" sneered Freddy Muldoon. "By the time he gets it he'll be commanding a supply base somewhere in Alaska."

"I know how to get to Colonel March," said Mortimer. "It's easy."

"How's that?" asked Jeff, as we all turned to look at Mortimer.

"It just takes a little brains, that's all," said Mortimer. "Not the kind Henry has...but somebody's got to do the non-scientific thinking for this club."

"I can't think of anybody better qualified," said Homer. "Let's hear it!"

Half an hour later we were all on our bikes, heading for the main gate of Westport Field. We had a lot of signs with us, with silly sayings like: "JOIN THE AIR FARCE!"..."UNCLE SAM DOESN'T WANT *YOU!*" ..."SUBMARINE FOR SALE, CHEAP!"...and "ONE OF YOUR CYLINDERS IS MISSING!" When we got there, we started doing a figure-eight in front of the guard house at the gate, waving the signs in the air, and singing "Anchors Aweigh!" All, except Mortimer. He got off his bike and started snapping pictures of the guard house and the gate with a camera that didn't have any film in it.

Two of the Air Policemen on guard at the gate came out and tried to stop us, but we just circled down the road a bit, and came right back when they went back in the guard house. Finally, one of them got on the phone, and pretty soon an Air Police van pulled up at the gate and a sergeant got out of it. He walked up to us and stood right in the middle of the road while we did the figure-eight around him. Freddy Muldoon got a little too close to him, and he reached out and grabbed Freddy's bike by the handlebars.

"Say, Fatty!" said the sergeant. "You wouldn't happen to have a banana on you, would you?"

I'd never seen Freddy Muldoon's Adam's apple before, but I saw it this time. It fluttered up and down his throat like a yo-yo. "I don't know what you're talkin' about," said Freddy. "My mother won't let me eat bananas. They make me burp."

"Are you tellin' me!" said the sergeant. "I can still smell 'em."

"In that case, you won't mind me leavin'," said Freddy. And he managed to wrench his bike free of the sergeant's grasp and scooted off down the road toward town.

Meanwhile, one of the other Air Policeman had managed to grab Mortimer by the collar and take his camera away from him.

"Shucks!" said Mortimer. "I shoulda known better."

"If you don't get out of here, I'm gonna take you to the base commander's office!" said the sergeant, standing in front of Mortimer with his hands on his hips. He looked as though he were seven feet tall.

"*You wouldn't dare!*" said Mortimer, pushing his chest

right up against the sergeant's belt buckle. "I got my rights!"

"What you've got is a big mouth!" said the sergeant. "Get in that van!"

By this time, the rest of us had gotten off our bikes and gathered around the sergeant, offering Mortimer moral support.

"Don't let him push you around, Mortimer."..."Tell him off!"..."He's not really as big as he looks!"..."Don't worry! We'll get you out."..."Hey, Sergeant! Your mouth is open!"

"Get in that van!" the sergeant ordered, grabbing Mortimer by the elbow. "And the rest of you, too!"

"You can't do this to me!" screamed Mortimer. "I'm an American citizen!"

"So am I!" said the sergeant. "Now get in there!" And he pushed him in.

He didn't have to push the rest of us. We jumped into the van like scared rabbits, and a few minutes later we were being herded into the Base Headquarters building where Colonel March had his office.

"What's all this?" asked a young lieutenant, sitting at a desk outside Colonel March's door.

"These are the kids that were demonstrating at the main gate," said the sergeant. "One of them claims to be an American citizen. I don't know about the rest of 'em."

"We didn't do nothin'," said Dinky Poore. "We were just protesting!"

"My! They do look pretty dangerous," said the lieutenant, knitting his brow into a frown. "That'll be all, Sergeant. Thank you."

"Yes, sir!" said the sergeant, saluting smartly. Then he

did an about-face, and walked out of the office like a ramrod, except he had to duck his head when he went through the door.

The lieutenant pressed a lever on the intercom on his desk. "Colonel, sir, there are five or six young citizens out here that I think you wanted to see."

"Yes! Send them in!" came the crackling response.

"Right this way!" said the lieutenant, as he held open the door to the colonel's office.

There, behind a huge mahogany desk, sat the colonel, and at first I didn't recognize him because he didn't have his hat on. But we all recognized the two men sitting in leather armchairs right beside the colonel's desk. They were Mr. Jenkins and Mr. MacComber.

"Well, this is indeed a pleasure," said the colonel, rising from his chair and extending his hand. "I think I recognize you young gentlemen. How on earth did you get through the gate?"

At this, everybody laughed, and we got sort of red in the face, and the colonel came around and shook all our hands while he got the lieutenant to bring more chairs into the office.

"I understand you wanted to see me about something," said the colonel, after we had all been seated. "I hear they call you the Mad Scientists of Mammoth Falls."

We all sort of looked at each other, and nobody seemed to know what to say. Finally, Henry managed a timid "Yes, sir."

"Tell me about this plan of yours. You're Henry Mulligan, aren't you?"

"Yes, sir! Well…it's really pretty simple…It just sort of came to me…And I thought, maybe…."

While Henry was doing his best to explain his idea, the colonel pressed a button on his intercom and said: "Send Major Cramer in here." In a few minutes an Army major with Engineer insignia on his lapels came in and took a chair.

When Henry had finished, the colonel asked him: "How far down did you say this cave was?"

"About fifty feet, sir."

"Find out what the pressure is at that depth, Major."

"I will," said the major, making a note.

"That would be about one-and-a-half atmospheres, sir," said Henry.

"Well...check on how much air pressure we'd need to get that water out of there, Major."

"About twenty-three pounds would do it," said Henry. "And it's really not a very big cave. I imagine you've got big enough compressors on that Army dredge to do the job, and...."

"Is there anything else you need to know, Major?" said Colonel March, with a big grin on his face.

And everybody laughed again, and Mr. MacComber, as usual, got caught with his cigar in his mouth and sprayed ashes and bits of tobacco all over Colonel March's desk.

"Boy! I can see right now, this is gonna cost me a lot of hamburgers," he said, when he had stopped choking.

"Now!" said the colonel, running his fingers through the thick mane of wavy white hair on his head. "I didn't get this white hair by running away from problems. And I didn't get it by not taking chances, either. I've been shot down twice in my career—once over Bremerhaven, and once over North Korea—so I know what it feels like. Incidentally, there's a saying in our business: 'The last time you get shot down, you don't even feel it!' "

The colonel laughed, and everybody laughed with him, but there was a different tone to it this time.

"Anyway...I don't know whether I should stake my career on a scheme dreamed up by a group called the Mad Scientists of Mammoth Falls...but the fact is, I've got just two days to get that bomb out of there...or this town is going to have an awful mess on its hands. So, I'm going to give it a try!"

"Whoopee!" cried Dinky Poore. "Excuse me, sir."

"That's all right, son. But don't get all excited. We may not be able to pull it off. It's just that I think it's the best plan I've had suggested to me, so far, so we'll give it a try. 'Might as well get shorn for a sheep as a lamb!'...as the saying goes."

"Can we print that, Colonel?" said Mr. MacComber.

"You mean the part about the sheep?"

"I mean the whole ball of wax. I mean, these kids were right about where the bomb was. Now you're gonna take their advice about how to get it out of there. I think it's a great story."

"It's a great story, all right, if it works," said the colonel. "But what if it doesn't? It would make me look pretty foolish...and it wouldn't make the Mad Scientists' Club look so good, either. After all, it isn't fair to ruin their reputations, too, is it?" And the colonel winked at Henry.

"I see what you mean," said Mr. MacComber.

"I'm afraid I'll have to ask your cooperation on that," the colonel went on. "If we get the bomb out, you can print the whole story. But right now, we're just working on a theory. And any scientist knows a theory is no good until you've proven it. Right, Henry?"

"That's right, Colonel...sir," said Henry. "There's just one other thing, though...could we possibly...."

"Absolutely not!" said the colonel. "I know what you're going to ask. But, I'll tell you what." And he winked at Mr. Jenkins. "If you want to set up that spy camera of yours up in the hills, like you did before, I'll send a communications sergeant along with you, and you can keep in touch with me by radio...just in case I need any advice."

"Whoopee!" said Dinky Poore. "Excuse me, sir."

"That's all right, son. Now, if you gentlemen will excuse me, we have to get moving. We only have two days, and a good part of this one is gone already."

After shaking hands with the colonel, and thanking him, we tore out of there and ran all the way to the main gate without even waiting for the lieutenant to call for the AP van to take us back. The APs at the gate had stacked our bicycles behind the guard house, and while we were pulling them out, the tall sergeant showed up in the van.

"Hey!" he hollered. "Do you mind if I confiscate those signs you brought with you? We're having a fan dancer at the NCO Club tonight, and I thought I might be able to use them."

"Sure!" said Mortimer, tossing the signs at him. "I'll even autograph one for you."

Then we pedaled off down the road as fast as we could, heading for Jeff's barn.

"By the way!" the sergeant shouted after us. "Give my regards to Banana Fats, will you?"

"Okay!" Mortimer hollered back at him. "Give my regards to the fan dancer!"

As we pedaled through town it was evident that the mood of Mammoth Falls had changed. American flags were flying in front of nearly every house and store front, and there were signs and banners everywhere saying things like: "GET OUT OF THE MARCH HAIR!"...and "DRAIN OUR LAKE AND WE'LL SHUT YOUR WATER OFF!"...and "DOWN WITH THE DEPARTMENT OF THE INFERIOR!"...and "WE'LL NEVER LET WASHINGTON SLEEP, HERE!" There was even one little sign on a house that said: "HENRY MULLIGAN FOR PRESIDENT!" Charlie Brown had organized a public meeting in front of the bandstand in the town square and he was urging people to write to everybody including the Pope to intercede and save the lake. And we heard that Abigail Larrabee had been on the radio pleading for women all over the country to come to Mammoth Falls and form a petticoat blockade around the lakeshore. Suddenly, all fear of the bomb and radiation had disappeared, and people were only concerned about Strawberry Lake. Instead of a heel, Colonel March had become a hero.

Mr. MacComber was true to his word. He and Mr. Jenkins showed up at our clubhouse with enough hamburger patties and rolls to feed a platoon, and an outdoor cook stove, to boot. Along with them came an Air Force sergeant named Skidmore, but when he introduced himself he said: "Just call me Sparky. Everybody else does." He had with him an Air Force jeep with a command net radio mounted in it.

"Let's get moving," said Freddy Muldoon. "I'm hungry!"

"I guess that's a good enough reason," said Mr. MacComber.

We all piled into the station wagon and the two jeeps

and headed for the old zinc mine. With the help of the sergeant's jeep we had an easier time getting the generator up the last leg of the road to the crusher, and Shorty got to ride with his camera cradled on his lap. Freddy and Dinky were really more interested in the cookout than they were in whether the bomb was recovered, so they helped Mr. MacComber cook hamburgers while the rest of us set up the TV equipment on the catwalk. Sergeant Skidmore drove his jeep into the brush right underneath us and jacked in two lines for a speaker and a mike so we could talk to Colonel March right from the catwalk. Before we'd finished setting up we could already see the patrol boats and the big Army barge with all its dredging equipment, about halfway across the lake, heading for the peninsula.

We were even more excited than the day before, because this time we felt we had a part in the operation. We worked like beavers getting the equipment set up, and then discovered we'd fallen into the old Army trap of "hurry up, and wait." There just wasn't anything to do but sit there and stare at the lake, and munch hamburgers and sip soda pop, while we watched the boats move into position off the peninsula. Dinky was wearing himself out climbing up the ladder with two hamburgers at a time, and finally Sergeant Skidmore got a helmet out of his jeep, tied a piece of commo wire to the chin strap, and used it for a hoist to bring up six or eight at a time.

"Brilliant, Sergeant! Positively brilliant!" said Mr. MacComber. "Where'd you get the idea?"

"Off the top of my head," said the sergeant.

Mr. MacComber gave us another one of his belly-rumblers. "You know, Sergeant, when I was in World

War II, the most useful thing we had was that old steel pot. You could cook a great stew in it, or take a bath, or use it for a seat, or raise geraniums in it when you were in reserve."

"Yeah! I've heard about that," said the sergeant.

"You ain't heard it all," said Mr. MacComber. "You know, sometimes our water ration was only half-a-canteen a day. We'd pour it into the old steel pot, and the first thing we'd do was brush our teeth. Then we'd shave with it, and after that we'd wash our hands and feet. You know what we'd do with what was left?"

"What?" said Dinky Poore, his eyes as big as silver dollars.

"We'd use it to make the coffee!" said Mr. MacComber, cutting loose another one of his rumbling laughs.

"That's enough war stories, Mac," Mr. Jenkins hollered down. "You'd better come up here. Sparky's going to make contact with the colonel now."

Mr. MacComber hefted himself up the ladder and shook the catwalk a bit when he flopped his big frame down beside the TV monitor. The boats had gotten into position, and Shorty had zeroed his camera in on the deck of the patrol boat he figured Colonel March was on. He zoomed in and picked up the colonel talking to Major Cramer on the rear deck. Sergeant Skidmore called in to the radio operator on board and told him we were all set up. We could hear the radio operator tell the colonel, "Remote unit in position and contact established, sir." Colonel March turned and waved in our direction, and everybody on the catwalk cheered. I felt something like an electric shock run down my spine. It was really exciting. It was like watching a football game on TV and being able to talk to the quarterback and tell him what to do.

Then there was another long wait. Finally we saw Colonel March move toward the pilot house, and the radio squawked. The colonel wanted to talk to Henry.

"We just want to let you people know that we're all set and ready to begin pumping," said the colonel. "We've sent divers down and have the hose secured in the cave. We'll soon know whether we can pull this off."

"Thank you, sir," said Henry. And we all sat back to watch and wait.

And it was a long wait…just like the day before, only this time we felt more involved in what was going on. We fussed and fidgeted, and made small talk, while we kept our eyes glued to the monitor. After what seemed like an hour, we saw two divers go over the side again, and we figured they must have finally pumped enough air into the cave to force the water out. But still we heard nothing on the radio.

"Maybe we ought to call the colonel," said Homer Snodgrass.

"Sorry!" said Sergeant Skidmore. "But the colonel told me definitely, 'Don't call me—I'll call you.' "

Just then, the colonel called.

"Gentlemen," he said. "I don't know what the trouble is, but we're not making any progress."

"You mean you don't have the water out of the cave yet?" Henry asked.

"That's right," said the colonel. "I don't understand it. We get pressure for awhile, and then we lose it. Maybe this won't work, Henry."

"It *should* work! It's *got to* work!" Henry insisted.

"I'm sorry, Henry. But something's wrong. We've sent the divers down to see if they can find any leaks in the hose."

Henry pondered that one for a minute. "I don't understand," he said finally. "Are there any bubbles coming to the surface?"

"I don't believe so. At least, I haven't seen any."

"You'd probably get a few big bubbles if you're getting pressure. But, if there's a leak in the hose there should be a steady stream of bubbles coming up. I don't understand it."

"I don't either," said the colonel. "But I'll check on that."

There was another long wait while we watched the colonel conferring with Major Cramer. Then the two divers came up and there was a lot of nodding and shaking of heads as they all talked together. Finally the colonel came back on the radio.

"Let me talk to Henry."

There was no answer, and we all looked around for Henry. We saw him at the end of the catwalk with his back against the wall of the crusher, gazing up into the trees.

"Yes, sir," he said, when we got him back to the mike.

"Henry, we don't know what's wrong. The divers say there's no leak in the hose. I'm afraid it just isn't going to work."

"It's *got to* work!" Henry repeated.

"Well...we'll give it another try, Henry. But it's after four o'clock, and I wouldn't want to get caught in the middle of this operation when it gets dark."

"Don't bother," said Henry. "Don't bother. There's something I've got to do."

"What do you mean, Henry?" the colonel asked.

But Henry had walked away, and we all watched in

amazement as he wrung his hands and kicked the wall of the crusher. Mr. MacComber walked up to him and patted him on the shoulder.

"I don't mean this to sound funny, Henry...but it looks as though your bubble has burst."

Henry turned and looked at him in a very funny way. "You know, Mr. MacComber...you may be exactly right!"

Then he turned to Mr. Jenkins, and there was a pleading look in his eyes. "Mr. Jenkins, could you drive me over to the State University right away? I've got to get there just as fast as I can."

"Well...sure, Henry. But I don't understand what's going on. Aren't you going to wait and see if they have better luck on the next try?"

"They won't have," said Henry. "We've only got one chance, and we've got to take it. The time is getting short! Please drive me over to the university!"

"Whatever you say, Henry!" said Mr. Jenkins, shrugging his shoulders.

And he and Henry took off to scramble straight down the hill to where we had left the station wagon.

The Final Strata-Gem

I wish I could have been with Henry on his visit to the State University, but he and Mr. Jenkins left so suddenly nobody even had a chance to ask why they were going there. So I can only give you Mr. Jenkins's account of what happened.

It's only about fifteen miles to the State campus, and he and Henry were probably there before the rest of us had packed up and gotten all our stuff back down the hill. They went straight to the office of Dr. Igor Stratavarious, who is a world-famous geologist. In case you never heard of him, he's the one who developed the theory that the continent of Atlantis did *not* sink into the ocean, as most historians and geologists have always claimed. Professor Stratavarious maintains that Atlantis is just where it always was, and that the rest of the world sort of grew up around it, and eventually it became covered with water. Other scientists keep challenging him to present proof of his theory, but he always says, "How about proving yours first? Show me the continent of Atlantis, and I'll show you an ivory tower full of fools!" He's a great favorite with the press, because he occasionally gets off a good one like that, and makes the rest of the scientific world look a little silly.

Anyway, Professor Stratavarious wasn't at his office. He was still lecturing to a class of two students over at the university assembly hall, and Henry and Mr. Jenkins tracked him down there. Henry didn't want to interrupt the lecture, of course, but after it had gone on for more than half an hour, and it was after five o'clock, he started waving his hand in the air to attract the professor's attention. The professor would adjust the monocle in his one good eye—he lost the other one during a revolution in Romania, and this is what decided him to come to America, where he claims people are better shots, and for this reason some of his students call him Cyclops—then he would smile and wave back at Henry, and gesture for him and Mr. Jenkins to take a seat in the class. This went on for another fifteen minutes, until one of the two students crept out of his seat and scampered up the aisle all bent over, as if he had to get to the bathroom in a hurry. The professor abruptly picked up the notes he had been lecturing from and slapped the lectern with them.

"Und dzo, I weel continue ze lectchaire on Tuesday," he concluded. Then he stalked off the stage and extended his hand to Henry.

" 'Enry, my good frand! What can I do for you?"

Mr. Jenkins noticed the professor's accent was much less noticeable in conversation then when he was on the platform.

"Professor Stratavarious, you've got to help us," said Henry. "It's important. It's about the bomb!"

"What bomb, 'Enry?"

"The atom bomb...the one the Air Force lost."

"Oh! Have zey lost one? Zat is good. Zat is very interesting."

Mr. Jenkins couldn't believe his ears. "Don't tell me you haven't heard about it, Professor. Don't you read the papers?"

"Papers? What papers? Oh, you mean ze newspapers! No, I never read zem. Zey are so depressing. Everyzing is always going wrong. In my country we have a saying: 'No news is good news.' So every week ze government puts out a newspaper...it is just a big, blank piece of paper zat says 'NO NEWS TODAY' in big letters. You can buy one if you want, but almost nobody does. Ze government finds szings run much smoother zat way." Then the professor burst into a hearty laugh and clapped " 'Enry" on the back, and " 'Enry" told him all about how the bomb had been lost, and how we had found it, and how the Air Force couldn't get it out of the cave, and about how the all the town was worried about the radiation, and about the draining of the lake, and everything.

"Ah, so!" said the professor. "Perhaps zat explains why I have had so few students zis week. You know, Mr. Jenkins, I usually have many more. Maybe five or six, sometimes."

"Seriously, Professor, I need your help," Henry explained. "You know the rock formations and substrata in this area like the back of your hand, and we need to find out...."

" 'Enry!" the professor interrupted. "Put your hands

behind your back, please."

Henry did so.

"Now tell me, 'Enry, what ze back of either hand looks like!"

"I...I don't really know," Henry stammered. "I can't describe it."

"Exactly!" said the professor. " 'Enry, I have told you, time and time again, zat in science we must be *precise*. We must know precisely what we are saying. So don't use stupid expressions like zat. If you want to say I know zis area like I know my own grandmother, zat is a little closer to ze truth...but it is still a stupid statement."

Mr. Jenkins walked over to a dark corner of the assembly hall and fanned himself with his hat. What would Henry get him into next, he wondered? When he walked back again within earshot of the two, the professor was stroking his chin whiskers and nodding his head thoughtfully.

"Zat is very interesting, 'Enry! *Very* interesting! Und dzo! Now we must find where ze air is going to. Correct?"

"Yes, sir! And we *must* hurry!"

"Science takes its own time, 'Enry," said the professor. "But we will give it ze old Bucharest College try, as you say in zis country! Hokay?"

"Hokay!" said Henry.

"First, we will go to my laboratory and decide which geological charts we should take wiz us. Zen, we shall go to your laboratory and look at zis engineer's map you have told me about. Hokay?"

"Hokay!" said Henry. "Only, I wish you wouldn't call it a laboratory."

"Never mind! I can be more precise after I have seen it. Zen, we must make an accurate survey. Hokay?"

"Hokay!" said Henry.

"Hokay!" Mr. Jenkins chimed in. "But let's get moving. I've got to file a story, and poor Colonel March...."

"Ho, yes!" said the professor. "I almost forgot. You must tell ze people about all ze trouble...right?"

"I guess you could put it that way," Mr. Jenkins grunted.

"Hokay!" said the professor. "Hokay! We go!" And he led the way out of the assembly hall.

On the way to the professor's laboratory, Henry filled Mr. Jenkins in on what was going on.

"You see," he said, "when they kept losing pressure in the cave, and yet the colonel said he didn't think there were any air bubbles coming to the surface, I knew there was something radically wrong. It couldn't happen. But it did. There just had to be another air passage out of that cave that was letting the pressure escape. The big problem is: How do you find it? Do you see?"

"Oh, sure! I see!" said Mr. Jenkins.

"Now, I've read that underwater caves were originally formed, sometimes, by underground springs. You know. As the water flows out of them it gradually erodes the ground away."

"Sure! Sure!"

"So, naturally, I thought of Professor Stratavarious. He's had his geology classes making diggings around this area for years, and he's developed the best geological profiles of the substructure in this part of the state that you'll find anywhere."

"Naturally! Naturally!"

"So, if there's any chance at all of finding out where

that air is escaping to, he's the one man who can do it. It's a long chance, but it's the only thing we can do."

"It's a long chance, all right," said Mr. Jenkins. "But even if you find where the air is going…what are you going to do about it?"

"I don't know," said Henry. "But I'll think of something."

"I'm sure you will!" said Mr. Jenkins. Then he laughed out loud. "You know…if it turns out to be a hole in the ground somewhere, you might try stuffing Freddy Muldoon into it, and just keep feeding him bananas until the leak stops."

That night was one of the wildest we've ever had around our clubhouse. Professor Stratavarious had brought a regular mountain of charts and maps with him, and he and Henry kept crawling around on the floor with calipers and magnifying glasses, looking for things that we couldn't even pronounce the names of. The rest of us sort of stood around and helped spread charts out on the floor, or roll them up again when the professor was finished with them.

"Look for water-bearing strata, 'Enry. Zey're in blue," he said. "By ze way, how deep did you say zat cave was?"

"About fifty feet," said Henry.

"Let's see! Zat would be…zat would be…let me see… we need ze watershed charts for ze last ten thousand years. Oh, my, my! I forgot ze watershed charts!"

Four times that night Mr. Jenkins drove the professor back to the university to get something he had forgotten. And Mr. MacComber would keep running downtown to get cold drinks and snacks. And Jeff's mother would keep running in with cocoa and coffee. Our clubhouse looked like the floor around an automatic vending machine. It was a mess!

Professor Stratavarious had a funny habit. If anybody said anything to him over his shoulder, he would spin around with his eyes popped open, and his monocle would drop out of his left eye. He would catch it on the toe of his shoe before it could hit the floor, with an expertise that was strictly automatic. One time Mr. MacComber tapped him on the shoulder to offer him some coffee, and the monocle plopped right into the cup.

"Excuse me, Professor! That was clumsy of me," said Mr. MacComber.

"Zat is no problem," said the professor, sticking his fingers into the hot coffee to retrieve the monocle. "Coffee is a good cleaning agent. If you don't believe it, spill some on your kitchen floor, and see. Ouch! Zat smarts! Ze trouble comes when ze monocle hits ze floor. You can't buy a new one anymore. Last time I broke one, it took eight months to get a new one from London."

And so it went. Henry and the professor kept checking back and forth from charts to maps and back to charts again, and then checking Henry's markings on the engineer's map of the county. The professor's theory was that the most likely escape route for the air was through a dried-up water-bearing stratum that formerly fed fresh water into the cave. The point of the exercise was to determine what the watershed in the area looked like at the time the cave was formed, and then figure out which of the old water-bearing strata on the professor's charts represented the most likely possibility. Then they had to try and determine the point in the hills surrounding the lake where the terminus of that stratum might be located today. The professor explained, for everybody's benefit, that a water-bearing stratum was nothing but a place where an underground stream of water could run downhill, and a terminus was just a place where the water first went underground or came up out of it. We were all so tired that we didn't much care, and most of the fellows had gone home to bed by the time the professor stepped up to the county engineer's map and drew a red circle northeast of the lake.

"I sink zat is ze most likely possibility, 'Enry," he said. "But we must check it with a ground survey in ze morning."

Henry placed the point of his calipers inside the circle the professor had drawn. "I know there's a big quarry on the side of that hill, right there," he said. "Maybe we should look there, first."

"Zat's a very good possibility," said the professor. "You dig a big hole, you disturb ze natural watershed. Zat could be why zat stratum dried up."

"If our ground survey in the morning checks out, maybe we should go right up there," said Henry.

"Good idea," said the professor. "Why don't you do zat, 'Enry?"

"Me? What about you, Professor? I'll need your advice."

"I sink I should get some sleep, 'Enry. Good night!" And the professor pulled an old saddle off the wall, propped his head on it as he stretched out on the floor, and began snoring almost immediately. Then, without opening his eye, or breaking the rhythm of his snores, he plucked the monocle from his left eye socket and slipped it into the breast pocket of his coat.

At the break of dawn most of us were back at the club-house and Mr. MacComber brought coffee and hot chocolate with him, so we wouldn't have to wake up

Jeff's mother. He apologized for being a little late.

"I stopped at three different all-night coffee shops, and I couldn't get any of them to make up a tuna fish and peanut butter sandwich for Freddy," he said.

For the next three hours we were scrambling all over the foothills northeast of Strawberry Lake, helping Henry and the professor check the exact locations on the ground that they had gone over on the professor's charts the night before. The professor cut quite a picture, squinting through the eye-piece of a surveyor's transit, with his coattails flapping in the morning breeze, his monocle held between two fingers behind him, and a black homburg set at a jaunty angle on his head. "Ah, dzo!" he would say, after getting Henry to put the sighting stick in exactly the right place. Then he would make a note on his tablet and smooth his waxed moustache, which got mussed every time he leaned up to the transit.

" 'Enry!" said the professor, finally. "I sink zere is no doubt about it. Zat quarry up zere is ze *only* place where water feeding into ze cave could come from."

"The *only* place?" Henry asked.

"Ze *only* place!" the professor repeated. "I will stake my professional reputation on it!"

"Gee! That's great," said Henry. "It sure makes things a lot simpler."

"It sure does!" said Jeff. "So, what do we do now, Henry? Let's get up there and take a look. Maybe we'll find a hole, or a cave, or something."

"Supposing you did?" Mr. MacComber asked. "What if you did find a hole? What could you do about it? I don't understand what this is all about, Henry."

"Right now we couldn't do *anything* about it," said

Henry. "What we've got to do now, is get out to the air base and talk to Colonel March! It's already eight o'clock, and there isn't much time left."

Up the hill we went, with Jeff and Mortimer pushing Professor Stratavarious up the steep places, and Mr. MacComber huffing and puffing along behind, with only Freddy Muldoon to keep him company. When we got to the rim of the quarry, the professor spread his arms wide and exclaimed: "Look at zis, 'Enry! It is marvelous! What did I tell you!"

We all looked, and there was no doubt about it. It was marvelous! The walls of the quarry on all sides were punctured with holes, fissures, caves, and just plain lateral slits in the rock face, of every description.

"Zis is marvelous! Just marvelous!" the professor repeated. "Zis was a major distribution point for ze watershed in zis area. And it has been uncovered for me by zose peasant stonecutters. Zis is a major discovery. I shall come here and document every inch of it. I must szank you, 'Enry, for making me discover it. Professor Stratavarious shall lecture here for years and years to come!"

We all looked at Henry, and his face had almost dropped to his knees. "That's just fine, Professor," he complained. "But how do we know which hole leads to the cave where the bomb is?"

"Zat is for you to figure out, 'Enry," said the professor. "I have shown you where to look. Zat is all I can do for my students. How much you learn from what I have shown you, is up to you! Now, if you will excuse me, gentlemen, I must get back to my office and get ready for next week's lectures."

And the professor stalked off down the hill toward

Turkey Hill Road.

"You'd better go after him," Henry said to Mr. Jenkins, "and drive him back to the university."

"But what about you, Henry? What are you going to do?"

"I'm going to find out which one of those holes leads to the cave where the bomb is."

"Are you nuts, Henry?" said Jeff. "How can we possibly do that?"

"I have an idea," said Henry. "If Colonel March goes along with it, maybe they can get that bomb out of there before the day is over."

"If they don't, it's all over for Colonel March," said Mr. MacComber. "What's your idea, Henry?"

"If you can get me in to see Colonel March, I'll tell you all about it," said Henry.

"Follow me!" Mr. MacComber grunted. And he led the way, slipping and sliding down the hill after Professor Stratavarious.

Mr. Jenkins dropped us off at the air base and took the professor on to the university. This time there wasn't any problem getting into the air base. Mr. MacComber phoned Colonel March from the guard house at the gate, and a jeep showed up to escort us to his office. The lieutenant sitting outside his office was wearing a long chin and looked pretty glum, but he greeted us politely.

"The colonel's not in a good mood this morning," he said. "He's been on the phone with Washington for almost an hour already. If you have any bad news for him, I wish you'd just send it in a letter."

"I hope we have *good* news for him," said Mr. MacComber, "but I don't know what it is yet."

The lieutenant gave him a double-take, and looked at him as if he were a nut, as he ushered us into the colonel's office. Colonel March looked tired and worried, and I felt very sorry for him, but he did manage to smile as he gestured to us to sit down. Just as we did, Major Cramer, the Army Engineer, came in.

"I asked Major Cramer to join us," the colonel explained, "because I figured Henry probably had another one of his zany ideas he wanted us to listen to. Fire away, Henry. You can't tell me anything sillier than what I've been hearing from Washington all morning."

Then Henry explained his theory about why the air escaped from the cave, and how we had spent most of the night with Professor Stratavarious trying to determine whether an underground stream bed had once fed water into the cave where the bomb was, and about the walls of the quarry that looked like a piece of petrified Swiss cheese. Through it all, Mr. MacComber kept nodding his head and grunting in corroboration of everything Henry said.

"I'll admit it's a long shot—maybe the odds are one thousand-to-one against us," said Henry. "But we've got to do something. And if we could just find out whether one of those holes in the quarry wall really does lead to the cave...why you might be able to block it up with stones and mortar, and then maybe you could build up pressure in the cave."

Colonel March was sitting at his desk with his head between his hands. "How on earth could you ever find out which hole we should plug up?" he asked.

"That's where we need your help," said Henry.

"What do you want me to do...have men crawl down

all those holes and see where they come out?"

"No," said Henry. "It's much simpler than that." And he turned toward Major Cramer. "Sir, do you have chemical smoke and a smoke generator?"

Major Cramer looked at Colonel March with a puzzled expression. "Well," he said, "we don't happen to have any here in Mammoth Falls."

Suddenly, Colonel March's head came up out of his hands. A gleam came into his eyes, and he stood up. "How fast can you get a smoke generator here?" he practically thundered at Major Cramer, pointing his finger at him.

The major bolted out of his chair, out of habit, and stood at attention. "I can get one here from Aberdeen in a matter of two or three hours, if there is a plane available to bring it."

"There will be a plane available!" said the colonel. "Get on the phone!" And he picked the phone up off his desk and handed it to the major.

"Henry! I think I know what you have in mind, and it is a brilliant idea! We'll pump chemical smoke into that cave under pressure and see if it comes out of one of those holes in the quarry. Right?"

"Or anywhere else between the cave and the quarry," said Henry. "I think it would be a good idea to have a couple of helicopters fly over the area while you're doing the pumping. But you should have a team ready at the quarry to try and plug up the hole if that's where the smoke comes out. It's the most likely place, according to Professor Stratavarious."

Colonel March spoke into the intercom on his desk. "Get Major Appleton and Captain Cunningham in here right away!" he told the lieutenant. Then he turned to Major Cramer. "Tell Aberdeen to send two smoke generators. We can't afford any lost time, if one breaks down. And plenty of smoke, too. We don't know how much we'll have to pump in, before it comes out the other end."

"Make sure the smoke they send isn't soluble in water," Henry added. "That's important. And a bright orange color is best. It's easier to see."

"Henry, you think of everything!" said the colonel.

"That's what I keep telling people," said Dinky Poore.

Mr. MacComber rose to his feet. "Colonel, I think it's best if I get these kids out of here, now. You've got a lot of work to do, and a lot of orders to give. And I just want to let you know that I wish you every success in getting that bomb out of there. Not just for the sake of the people in this town, but for your own sake as well. Believe me, I know what you've been going through." And he stepped over and shook the colonel's hand.

"Thank you, Mr. MacComber," said the colonel. "And believe me, I have the feeling you'll get the story you want this time. If there's anything I can do for you, please let me know."

"We'll take care of ourselves all right, Colonel. I'll be wherever these kids are, 'cause I figure that's my big story. I should ask if there's something *I* could do for *you*, to help out in this business."

"Matter of fact there is," said the colonel. He dug into his pocket and spun a half-dollar toward Mr. MacComber. "Buy that fat kid enough bananas to get him through the day."

"I don't think half-a-buck will do it," said Mr. MacComber, "but I'll chip in with you."

From that point on, things really moved. We took off for our clubhouse, and Sergeant Skidmore soon showed up there with his jeep.

"The colonel says I'm to stay with you all day," he said. "He's already sent some men up to the quarry, and they're flying in a squad of Army mountain troops from Fort Carson. They should be here before noon."

Mr. Jenkins showed up, too, and we filled him in on what was going on.

"Sounds like a great idea, Henry," he said. "But it gives me a problem. I wanna be there to shoot that smoke coming out of the wall of the quarry…if it does…but I also want to get the recovery operation from the stone crusher. I'd better get another camera crew down here!"

Jeff took him into his house so he could telephone WEYE-TV in Clinton, and he came back to report that they would not only lend him a camera crew, but they were also chartering a helicopter to fly a cameraman over the area most of the day.

"That won't do them any good," said Jeff. "I'm sure the Air Force won't let anybody fly over the lake while they're recovering the bomb, and I'll bet they don't let any aircraft within five miles of here."

"That's for sure!" said Sergeant Skidmore. "This has been a restricted air zone all week."

"I realize that," said Mr. Jenkins. "But if I hadn't suggested that to them, they might not have loaned me the camera crew."

"What do we do now, Henry?" said Mr. MacComber.

"I guess we can just relax and enjoy the show," said Henry. "I don't really know what else to do. It's all up to the Air Force, now. But I won't really relax until I see some orange smoke come out of one of those holes up there in the quarry."

"That's for me, too!" said Jeff. "Let's get up there. If your idea works out, and they do get that hole plugged up, we'll have plenty of time to get over to the zinc mine and watch the recovery operation."

"Wait a minute," said Mr. Jenkins. "I can't get my station wagon up to that zinc mine to get my equipment set up. I'll need your help."

"Okay!" said Jeff. "I'll go with you and we can take our jeep and the generator. But let's get moving. Maybe I can get back to the quarry in time."

"You still got about two hours," Sergeant Skidmore told him. "They don't expect those smoke generators in till about noontime."

By noontime, both Jeff and Mr. Jenkins had joined us at the quarry, and Shorty the cameraman was left at the stone crusher with Dinky to keep him company and help him set up his camera equipment. They told us the recovery crew had been in action since ten-thirty, and they had just seen another boat leaving the town dock, where a big Air Force truck was parked. They figured this might be the boat taking the smoke generators out to the Army barge.

"Hot dang!" exclaimed Homer. "Maybe we'll see some action pretty soon."

We did. Somehow the word seemed to have gotten around town that something was going on up at the quarry, and we began to see little groups of people straggling up the hill, gaping over the rim of the quarry, and asking the airmen and soldiers lounging around if they knew what was going on. Like most soldiers, nearly all of them said, "Beats me, Mac! If you find out, how about letting me know?"

Pretty soon, even Mayor Scragg and Charlie Brown struggled up the hill with a few other members of the Town Council, and they seemed to know what was going on, because they didn't ask any questions. We knew, of course, that Colonel March had a liaison officer at the Town Hall whose only job was to keep the mayor informed of what the Air Force was doing.

The radio in Sergeant Skidmore's jeep crackled, and the sergeant ran over and answered the call. It was Colonel March, letting us know that the smoke generators had arrived, and as soon as the engineers had them properly hooked into the compressor, and had run a few tests, they would be ready to start pumping smoke into the cave. The colonel estimated they'd begin sometime before one o'clock. We all corked off with a small cheer at this news and jumped up and down a bit, and people all around the quarry rim looked in our direction and some of them came wandering over.

The other airmen assigned to the quarry got the same message over the operations net, and we heard one of them relaying the information by walkie-talkie to the men they had stationed on the quarry floor. A lot of people gathered around him to hear what he was saying, and he had to ask them to stand back so they wouldn't push him over the edge. The Army squad of mountain troops began stirring around and checking all the climbing tackle they had laid out on the ground. Overhead, a big cargo-carrying chopper suddenly appeared and made a practice landing in an area where the airmen had cleared the scrub growth and rocks away and spread out nylon panels painted international orange. The place had suddenly come to life, and you could almost feel the electricity in the air.

I could feel something else, too. It was Mortimer, slapping me on the shoulder and gesticulating wildly toward the woods to the east of the quarry. From a narrow path among the trees emerged the figure of Professor Stratavarious, complete with black homburg and walking stick, and behind him straggled a motley assortment of students dressed in every conceivable kind of regalia...except that there wasn't very much of it on any of them. The professor marched the group right to the quarry's rim, and indicated with a sweep of his walking stick where they should seat themselves. Then he apparently became aware that they were not alone. He plucked the monocle from his eye, and stood with his hands on his hips, surveying the various groups of people gathered around the chasm. Then he swung round to face his students.

"You see! Ze place is already famous!" he practically shouted. "Someday you may come back here and find it is called Stratavarious Quarry." Then he proceeded to lecture the class on the geological features exposed on the quarry walls and paid no more attention to the people around him.

In a few minutes, the radio crackled again. It was Colonel March, telling us that they were ready to begin pumping. I felt my heart beat pick up, and then it started to thump, and I guess everybody else's did, too. We all instinctively moved to the rim of the quarry and peered into it, trying to keep our eyes on all the holes at the same time. This was obviously stupid, so we quickly split up in pairs and took positions at different places on the rim so that we could concentrate on the south and west walls of the quarry. Henry and I plopped down together and shared a pair of field glasses I had brought with me.

On the floor of the quarry, and at various places around the perimeter, the airmen and soldiers were doing the same thing, plus a lot of other things. Three teams of men were walking along the edges of the quarry, dangling smoke detectors over the side on the ends of long cords. And on the floor three more teams were scanning the walls with detectors mounted on long poles.

The minutes just crawled by, as they do in such situations, and my heart just kept on thumping. The airmen kept walking the rim and the floor of the quarry, sweeping their smoke detectors past the face of every hole they could reach. The curiosity-seekers who had come to see what was going on, kept shifting their eyes from one hole to another as fast as they could, hoping not to miss anything. And Professor Stratavarious kept lecturing his class, stabbing his walking stick at the great maw of the quarry as he talked.

The operations net radio squawked several times, as an officer on one of the patrol boats wanted to know if any smoke had been sighted, and the communications sergeant replied negatively each time.

Then, suddenly, an airman on the floor of the quarry shouted, "I'm getting a reading, Sergeant! I'm getting a reading!"

Everyone's eyes turned toward the southwest corner of the quarry, where the airman stood with his smoke detector held to the mouth of a jagged hole about twenty feet up the quarry wall.

"Are you sure?" the sergeant shouted back from his perch on the rim. "Check it out! Harrison! Get over there and see if you can confirm that reading! I don't see anything."

One of the other airmen stumbled over the rocks on the quarry floor to get his detector over the same hole. But before he got there, a faintly yellowish vapor became visible. Slowly, it changed in density and color, until there was no doubt about it. A curling wraith of bright orange smoke was rising up the quarry wall!

A tremendous cheer went up from the rim of the chasm and echoed back and forth between the walls. By the time it had died down, the wraith of smoke had become a thick, billowing cloud, spreading slowly in every direction. Professor Stratavarious had spun around at the sound of the cheering, and stood silhouetted against the sky with his arms outspread...the monocle in one hand and the walking stick in the other. In the silence following the echoes of the cheer, he cried out:

"I have discovered a volcano! I have discovered a volcano!"

The radios crackled again as both Sergeant Skidmore and the sergeant in command of the troops called in to say, "Cut the smoke! Cut the smoke! We've found it! We've found it!"

Henry and I were jumping up and down and hugging each other, and on the other side of the quarry we could see Mayor Scragg and Charlie Brown shaking hands with each other and with the other members of the Town Council. Even the people who didn't know what was going on seemed to know that something momentous had happened.

We raced back to Sergeant Skidmore's radio in time
to hear Colonel March say, "Tell Sergeant Adams we
won't cut the smoke off until you're certain the smoke
is coming out of only one hole. We don't have time to
make any mistakes."

Sergeant Skidmore hollered over to Sergeant Adams,
who was already getting the same message over the
operations net, and Sergeant Adams hollered back to
him, "Okay! Okay! We'll double-check it!"

We all peered over the rim as the smoke continued to
billow out of the hole, and there was no doubt about it.
The smoke was only coming out of one hole.

"Good!" said Colonel March, when this information
was reported back to him. "That makes the job simpler.
We'll cut off the smoke. Get that hole plugged up, and
let us know when to put the pressure on. Now, get
cracking! We don't have all day!"

"Roger, sir!" said Sergeant Skidmore. And we
could hear Sergeant Adams already starting to crack
out the orders. "Okay! Mountain troops! Over the
side! Get that scaffold slung! Hop to it! Let's move!
Commo Sergeant! Order up the first chopper, and
stand by!"

The place sprang alive. Men started running all over
the place, and the mountain troops began seating
grappling hooks and slinging lines over the side.
Something that looked like a painter's scaffold was
lowered down to the hole, and two men scrambled
down the wall on ropes. Others on the quarry floor
were gathering rocks and loading them into buckets
slung on ropes from the rim. It was only two minutes, it
seemed, before we heard the throbbing of the big chopper. And when it appeared over the trees, two airmen

guided it to a sitting-duck landing in the prepared clearing. Out of it came buckets of freshly-mixed, quick-setting cement, which were immediately carried to the rim of the quarry and lowered over the side. The two men on the scaffold worked like beavers, jamming rocks into the gaping hole and tamping wet cement around them.

It wasn't long before the hole had been filled up and the front of it looked like a smooth plaster wall. Then the men inserted a variety of small, sharp objects into the cement and hooked wires to them.

"What on earth are those?" I asked Henry.

"I can only guess," said Henry. "But I imagine those are sensors. Some of them are probably moisture detectors and temperature gauges, so they can tell when the cement has dried. Then, I'd bet they've put some strain gauges in there. If they didn't, they'd better. Because, when they start to pressurize that cave, they're going to have to know whether that cement job will hold the pressure."

Once the patch job had been done, there was no reason to hang around the quarry any longer...unless we wanted to see whether the patch blew out. So we all made our way back down the hill to Turkey Hill Road, and so did everybody else except the airmen and soldiers who had to stay there...and Professor Stratavarious, who just kept on lecturing his class, oblivious of the fact most everyone had left and the smoke had stopped pouring from the hole in the quarry wall.

"Well, Henry," said Mr. MacComber, as we picked our way down the hill. "We come to the moment of truth again. We'll soon know whether the textbooks are right, huh?"

Henry blushed a little. "Let's hope that was the only place the air was escaping. We haven't had any report from the helicopters that were supposed to be watching the area between here and the lake."

We soon did. Colonel March came on the radio as soon as we got to Sergeant Skidmore's jeep. He told us they were satisfied they could start pumping as soon as the cement in the hole was strong enough, and the engineers predicted it would be about another hour yet.

As soon as Mr. MacComber had filed his story at the Bristol Hotel, and Mr. Jenkins had sent his film off to Clinton, we made our third expedition up to the ore crusher at the old zinc mine. The place was beginning to feel like a second home to us.

"I hope this is the last time I have to climb up here," Mr. MacComber grunted, as he heaved his huge bulk from the top of the ladder onto the catwalk. "You know something? I forgot to bring any hamburgers."

Everybody laughed except Freddy, who pulled a banana from his shirt and made a big point of eating it ostentatiously in front of the rest of us.

"Is there anything you don't like to eat, Freddy?" Mr. Jenkins asked him.

"Yeah!" said Freddy. "The doctor says I should have more iron in my diet, but I have trouble chewing the stuff!"

Mr. MacComber laughed so hard he actually collapsed right on the catwalk and we had to help him to his feet and sit him down by the TV monitor.

True to the colonel's prediction, the pumping started right at two-thirty, and we all sat there with our eyes glued to the monitor. And for Henry's sake, we all kept our fingers crossed, praying the cement in the quarry wall would hold. The pumping went more slowly this time, and Colonel March called in to explain why. They were building the pressure slowly, and stopping periodically to get the strain gauge readings by radio from the crew at the quarry. We watched and we waited.

Finally, we saw a slight commotion on the deck of the patrol boat, and Colonel March stepped over and shook Major Cramer by the hand and clapped him on the back. Then he turned and ran to the pilothouse.

"Henry!" his voice came from the speaker beside us. "I should shake your hand, too! We think we have full pressure. We're sending divers down right away to check the cave. Cross your fingers, Henry!"

"That won't be necessary," Mortimer chirped. "My knuckles are white right now!"

I've tried holding my breath underwater, and I think the best I ever did was about two minutes. But I know I broke the record right there that afternoon, because it took the divers a lot longer than that to get down into that cave and back up again. But, when they did there were signs of jubilation on the deck of the patrol boat. We almost knew what the colonel would say when his voice came over the radio, but we kept our fingers crossed until we'd heard it.

"Henry, we've done it!" he practically shouted. "Or...maybe *you've* done it...I don't know...but the divers say the water is out of the cave, and we're ready to proceed. Keep your fingers crossed!"

"I can't! I can't!" screamed Mortimer. "I'm a nervous wreck already!"

The rest of the operation took about three hours, and it got pretty boring looking at the deck of the patrol boat, and the deck of the barge, and the surface of the water...trying to visualize what was going on fifty feet below. But the great moment finally arrived, and with a little advance notice from Colonel March, we watched intently as a definite turbulence became apparent on the surface of the water...and then two life rafts lashed around a crate bobbed to the surface and bounced up and down for a few seconds.

How the old catwalk on that ore crusher withstood it, I don't know, but we all leaped in the air at once and screamed and hollered and shouted and jumped up and down. Even Mr. MacComber got his heels off the floor as he clapped his hands. Everybody was pounding Henry on the back at once, and his knees started to buckle under him. Then the radio squawked.

"Henry! We've done it!" the colonel shouted. "From here on in, it's clear sailing. You can go home. I want to thank you, Henry, but I don't have time right now. Will you all come out to the air base at noontime, tomorrow?"

Henry could hardly answer, but Mortimer blurted out, "Yes, sir!" and he snapped off a smart salute to the TV monitor.

By the time we had gotten all of Shorty's stuff down from the crusher, and had made it into town, it was obvious everybody knew the bomb had been recovered. The streets were thronged with people hoping to get a glimpse of the truck that would undoubtedly have to carry the bomb from the town dock back out to the air base. They saw the truck, all right. But there wasn't any bomb in it, as we found out later. It wasn't that Colonel March wanted to fool anybody, but he was too smart to haul an atom bomb down the main street of any town. He had the Army Engineer barge take the bomb up to the northeast corner of the lake, where Jeff and Harmon and I had landed in the fog the day the bomb had plopped into the water. A truck waiting there took the "nuclear device" back to the air base. Meanwhile, the truck that had delivered the smoke generators to the dock paraded slowly through town, deadheading it back to the air base with two Air Police jeeps escorting it, to give the townspeople a thrill.

We were all so tired, by this time, that all we wanted to do was get home to bed. And the next thing I can remember is my mother jabbing my backsides with the kitchen broom.

"Get up, sleepyhead! You'll make me late for church!"

"Aw-rr-rr...what time...what time it is, Ma?"

"Do you mean what time *is* it?"

"Aw-rr-rr...I don't...Aw-rr-rr...Blooey!"

"You should know better than to ask a question like that! Anybody would think you were married to that mattress, the way you hold on to it. Get up and wash your face with some cold water."

"Aw, Ma!"

I didn't have the strength to get up, but I did manage to roll off the bed and onto the floor.

"You can do better than that," said my mother, jabbing me again with the broom. "Mr. Jenkins called, and he's going to be here at quarter-to-twelve to take you to Westport Field."

"Jeepers!" I cried, springing to my feet. "What time is it, Ma?"

"Quarter-to-twelve," she said, and went out of the room.

It wasn't, really, but it *was* eleven-fifteen, and I barely had time to get my hair slicked down and put on my best Sunday suit. When Mr. Jenkins arrived, there was an Air Force sedan along with him that had half the gang in it, so I got to ride out to the air base sitting up, instead of lying on the floor in the back of his wagon like I usually did.

We went straight to Colonel March's office, and he spent about fifteen minutes thanking us for all the help we had given him and joking about some of the funny things that had happened during the week.

"Now that it's all over," he said, "I can laugh a little bit about things like Mr. Okeby's watermelons, and the petticoat parades. The townspeople certainly did a good job of getting their message across to us. Now, if you'll follow me, gentlemen, we have some more formal business to take care of."

He led the way out of his office to a line of Air Force cars parked at the curb in front of the headquarters building. We rode in style, with a motorcycle escort leading the way, and pulled up in front of a building with a sign over the door saying: WESTPORT FIELD OFFICERS CLASS "A" MESS.

"They oughta take that sign down," said Dinky Poore. "I don't think they're that bad."

"You're a dumb nut!" said Freddy Muldoon. "A mess is a place where officers eat."

"Why can't they eat at a table like other people do?"

"Hoh, boy!" said Freddy, clenching his fists. "Hey! You know what? I betcha they're gonna feed us!"

That was an understatement. We were ushered into a huge dining room where about two hundred people were already sitting down at long tables set for a banquet, and when Colonel March led us to chairs at the

head table, everybody in the room stood up and
applauded. I felt like dropping through the floor, and I
know I was all red in the face, and so was everybody else
in the gang. My dream about the sword of Damocles
came back to me, and I instinctively locked my arms in
front of me to make sure my pants didn't fall off.
Colonel March made a short speech to welcome everybody, and explain that the luncheon was being held to
celebrate the recovery of the bomb, and also to honor
the members of The Mad Scientists of Mammoth
Falls...and all of us blushed bright red again, and all I
could do was look down at the floor. Then he invited
everyone to start eating, and waiters came streaming in
with everything from soup to toothpicks. Sure enough,
there was roast beef on the menu, and plenty of Jaspar
Okeby's watermelons, and I watched Freddy wolfing his
down, but I couldn't eat a bite.

Mayor Scragg and all the Town Council were there,
and Congressman Hawkins, and Abigail Larrabee, and
most of the reporters and photographers we had seen
in town; and there was an Air Force general with eight
inches of ribbons on his chest sitting at the head table
next to Colonel March, and a lot of other important-
looking people who were later introduced as officials
from Washington...including one who Colonel March
claimed was the acting deputy assistant under secretary
of the Air Force.

After everybody had stuffed themselves, the speeches
started, of course, and there were plenty of them. Every
speaker wanted to expound his own unique version of
the momentous thing that had happened; and the way
the bouquets and compliments were being passed back
and forth you'd never think the town had ever been

upset about anything at all. I had to go to the bathroom so bad my toes were aching, but I didn't dare get up out of my seat, so I just sat there gritting my teeth and sweating through it all. Dinky Poore had the best idea. He just fell asleep with his head on the table and nobody paid any attention.

Finally, Colonel March introduced the general, who got up and read a letter that he had sent to the Air Force Committee on Awards and Decorations recommending that all seven members of the Mad Scientists' Club be awarded the Medal for Meritorious Service for their part in locating and helping recover the bomb. And he said he had every confidence that the awards would be approved. Then everybody stood up and applauded and cheered, and several people hollered "Speech! Speech!" and we all looked at each other and jabbed our thumbs in Henry's direction. Henry was finally persuaded to get up on his feet, and he blushed and stammered a bit, but all he could think of to say was, "Thank you! And I hope you enjoyed your lunch." Then he sat down, and everybody clapped some more.

Then we were escorted out the door and Henry was asked to ride with Colonel March and the general in the fanciest jeep you ever saw. It had chrome wheels and bumpers, and three silver stars on it, and two blue flags on the fenders with three white stars. The rest of us were escorted to a flat bed Air Force truck all decorated with blue and yellow bunting and big signs on the sides that said: "WE LOVE YOU, MAMMOTH FALLS! WE LIVE HERE, TOO!" The next thing we knew, we were in a parade. We sat on a raised platform in the middle of the truck, surrounded by an Air Force honor guard, standing at attention. And we rolled into town with all kinds of vehicles and bands joining the procession as it moved. Mammoth Falls had never seen anything like it...and still hasn't...because there were so many people in the parade that there were only three or four people left over to watch it from the sidewalks...plus a pack of dogs. But it was fun, anyway, and we whooped and hollered and threw peanuts at the dogs as they ran along yelping and barking at everything passing by.

When it was all over, Mr. MacComber asked Mr. Jenkins to drive him to the county airport outside of Clinton so he could catch a plane to New York, and we all rode with them to see him off. On the way we had a great time comparing notes and jokes about all the events of the week, and Mr. MacComber practically had tears in his eyes when we finally pulled up at the airport passenger ramp. While we were all shaking hands and saying goodbye, Freddy Muldoon tapped Mr. Jenkins on the shoulder.

"Hey, Mr. Jenkins, could we stop at Mr. Parson's farm on the way back?"

"Well, I guess we could, Freddy. What for?"

"Well, he usually dresses his chickens for market on Sunday afternoon, and I want to see if I can get some chicken heads for my mother."

"Chicken heads?" Mr. MacComber gulped. Then he put his head between his hands and groaned. "Freddy! I know I shouldn't ask this...but what on earth can you do with chicken heads?"

"Ain't you never heard of chicken noodle soup?" said Freddy, gazing at him in wide-eyed wonder.

Mr. MacComber closed his eyes and bit down hard

on his cigar. He groped for Mr. Jenkins's hand and shook it.

"Jake!" he said. "Remind me never to come back here, will you?"

Then he picked up his bags and slouched off toward his plane, where he disappeared in the darkness beyond the doorway.

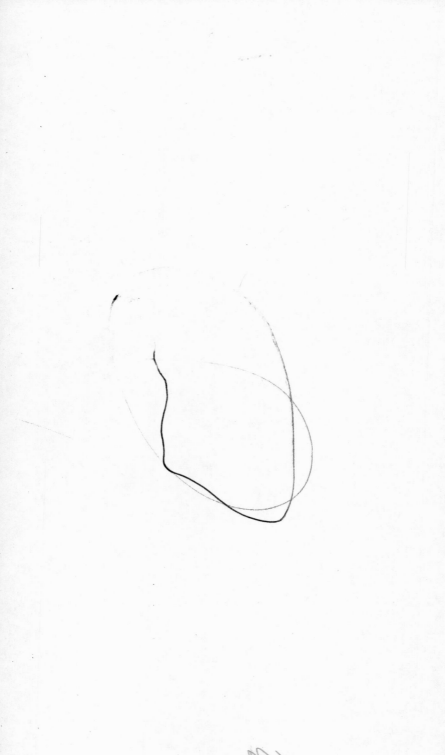